WHO IS FOSTER

ANN STROMSNESS

WESTBOW
PRESS®
A DIVISION OF THOMAS NELSON
& ZONDERVAN

WestBow Press books may be ordered through booksellers or by contacting:

WestBow Press
A Division of Thomas Nelson & Zondervan
1663 Liberty Drive
Bloomington, IN 47403
www.westbowpress.com
844-714-3454

All scripture quotations are taken from The Holy Bible, New International Version®, NIV® Copyright © 1973, 1978, 1984, 2011 by Biblica, Inc.® Used by permission. All rights reserved worldwide.

ISBN: 978-1-6642-6489-2 (sc)
ISBN: 978-1-6642-6490-8 (hc)
ISBN: 978-1-6642-6488-5 (e)

Library of Congress Control Number: 2022907697

Print information available on the last page.

WestBow Press rev. date: 05/23/2022

JUNE 2, 2011

Josiah Kanell sat at his desk in his office at First Community Church. He was busily taking notes as he listened to the person on the other end of the phone wedged between his shoulder and jaw. After several minutes, he said, "sounds good." He listened for another minute, then wished the caller a blessed day and hung up. With a sigh, Josiah leaned back in his chair and relaxed. He ran his fingers through his dark brown hair noticing it was getting a little long. He would need to get a haircut soon. His hair was naturally curly and tended to get unruly if he let it get very long. He glanced at the clock and was amazed to find it only read 10:22. Josiah served as youth pastor at First Community Church and had spent the last month planning the third annual retreat for the church's young people. The retreat was still 6 weeks away, but he had wanted to get the flyers out this week. Today was Thursday. He needed to leave the church by 1:00 today to go with his wife to her ultrasound and doctor's appointments. The birth of their second child was five and a half weeks away. And tomorrow was the long-awaited appointment with a specialist for their almost two-year-old daughter, Abigail. It was sure to take most of the day. So today was his last chance to finish up the plans for the retreat if the information was going to get to the young people by Sunday. He had been playing phone tag with the director of Camp Hope for two weeks. Finally, he had reached him this morning. With that phone call, all the details were in place. He just needed to insert the last bit of information into the brochure and give it to the church secretary to print. It was a relief to have it done and with time to spare. He brought up the brochure on his computer, filled in the information, and hit print. As it was printing, he prayed that the retreat would be attended by those teens who needed to be there and that they would grow spiritually as a result. He unfolded his six-foot four-inch frame from the desk chair and reached for the printed brochure. He headed out the door and down the hall to drop off the printed brochure to Roberta, the church secretary, to have additional copies made, folded, and distributed to the church mailboxes. They would be put in all the mailboxes even if the family didn't have a teen. They might know a teen. He also asked her to make an extra 25 copies hoping some of the young people would want to invite friends who didn't normally attend their church. Josiah had started the yearly summer retreat shortly after he joined the staff at First Community four years ago to spend some good quality time with the teens, ground them in God's word, and as an outreach opportunity. He had worked at Camp Hope during college and knew that the camp ran four weeks of camp from mid-June to mid-July for preteens and then took a week off before returning to run an additional four weeks of teen camps. The camp director was happy to let Josiah use the camp during those days off if they provided all their own staff. In the past, Josiah had directed the retreat and done all the teaching. He hoped to be able to do it this summer, but plans were a little uncertain with his wife's due date being 3 days before the start of the retreat. Abby had arrived two weeks late and Josiah and Kate had prayed about Josiah's involvement. Technically it was his responsibility, but another member of the church had offered to fill in. Since the camp was only forty-five minutes away, Kate had encouraged Josiah to plan to be at the retreat unless the doctor felt that she was ready to deliver. Josiah was torn. He enjoyed the time with the teens at the retreat but knew how tired Kate would be near the end and just how active Abby was. Both of their mothers lived close by, and his wife assured him if she was home from the hospital that they would manage just fine. Josiah wasn't sure what to do and prayed for wisdom and peace. About 12:30 with the brochure done, and plans for Sunday's youth group finished, Josiah decided to head for home a little early.

When Josiah reached home, he entered the apartment quietly. His wife, Kate, tried to rest when Abby napped. Abby would turn two years old tomorrow. She was a bright and active child who continually delighted her parents. She was also deaf. When she had failed her newborn hearing test, their pediatrician sent them for a full hearing evaluation. The audiologist who performed the test informed them that Abby was profoundly deaf and hearing aids were not an option. They should connect with services to begin sign language asap. Shortly after Abby's first birthday, she began to have ear infections one right after the other. They were referred to an ENT, ear nose, and throat doctor, for ear tubes. When they went in for their follow-up appointment, the ENT asked why Abby had never been evaluated for hearing aids. Josiah explained that the audiologist had told them hearing aids wouldn't help. The ENT had disagreed and referred them to a specialist. He said this specialist was very good and if anyone could help Abby he could. The downside was that because he was so good it would probably take at least six months to get an appointment. The specialist had run many tests and tomorrow's appointment was the day they would learn the results. When they finally got to see the specialist, he had agreed that hearing aids could help Abby. She probably wouldn't hear speech clearly but neither would she be living in a silent world. The big questions were if Abby's hearing loss was genetic, were there any other abnormalities to watch for, and what about the new baby? Tomorrow was the big day. They would receive the results of the genetic testing. And Abby would get her hearing aids.

As Josiah entered the living room, he spotted Kate and Abby curled up together in the recliner. He smiled as he saw Abby cuddled in her mom's left arm with her head resting on Kate's extended abdomen, her blond hair curling softly around her face. Her big blue eyes closed in slumber. Kate's light brown shoulder-length hair was down a hair tie around her wrist. He smiled- he could just picture Kate working around the apartment with her hair up in a ponytail. She would forget about the ponytail until she was settled in the recliner with Abby. Then when she put her head back, the ponytail would be uncomfortable. She would pull it out, putting the hair tie on her wrist for safekeeping Kate's left hand rested lightly on Abby's back, her right was on her stomach as if holding their growing child. This was their favorite place to nap. Abby had a hard time closing her eyes to rest unless she was touching someone. They guessed it might be that with her hearing loss she felt isolated when she couldn't see anything. Whatever the reason, she went right to sleep when curled up in the big recliner with either Kate or Josiah and struggled to get to sleep in her bed.

Josiah sat on the couch across from his sleeping wife and child and bowed his head to pray for today's ultrasound, the next day's appointment, and the upcoming birth. He was asking God to help them accept the doctor's news when he heard Kate stir. He looked up to see her watching him. "Love you," he said as he stood to kiss her.

"What time is it?" she asked sleepily "Is it time to go?"

"It's only about 1:00 so we have time," he answered.

"You're early," she said. "Did you reach the camp director?"

"Yes, finally, everything is set. How was your morning?" he asked.

"Busy, but I got a lot done for the party on Saturday," she answered.

Tomorrow was Abby's second birthday. Today was Joe's and Kate's birthdays. Their moms had been roommates in the hospital when they were born. Joe was three hours older than Kate. Joe's parents hadn't been Christians, but the two moms, each with their first baby had developed a friendship. About six months later Kate's mom, Ruth, had led Joe's mom, Joy, to the Lord. Joe's dad made a decision for Christ a few months later. The families spent a lot of time together growing up. Ruth and her husband Charlie Landers had identical twin boys, Zachariah and Ezekiel, 2 years after Kate on June 12th. Joy and Dan Kanell had had a girl, Karen, 2 days before the twins on June 10, 1985.

5

Most family gatherings usually included both families even before Josiah and Kate had married. None of the extended family lived locally except Charlie's older brother Herb who ran a small motel nearby. So, the families continued to get together often now as adults who still enjoyed each other's company. Everyone's birthdays were in June. With 11 people with birthdays in June the family always picked one Saturday to have a huge family birthday party. They would spend the day at a park on a local lake. This year the party was planned for June 4th. Zeke and his wife Leah (born June 14) were expecting their first child on June 21st. Zach and his wife Lydia (who was Leah's twin) were expecting their first child on June 28th. And Karen was getting married on June 18th to Eric Green. The family often teased good-naturedly that Joe and Kate missed it when they planned this baby. They should have had a June baby to match the rest of the family, not a July baby. They would tease that those three weeks between the rest of the birthdays and this little one's birthday was going to seem awful long to a small child. Joe teased back, you just want to be able to celebrate all our birthdays at the same time, so you don't have to remember when they are. Thinking of how tiring Saturday would be for his wife and how long tomorrow's appointment might be Josiah frowned.

"What's that look for?" Kate asked.

"What?" he asked.

"You were frowning," she said.

"Was I?" he asked.

"Yes," she stated, "most definitely you were."

"I was just thinking," he said as he sent up a quick prayer. "I wonder if maybe you should stay home and rest tomorrow. It's sure to take most of the day and Saturday is going to be tiring too. I don't want you to overdo it".

"I'll be fine," she reassured. "But if it will make you feel better, let's ask the doctor this afternoon. I'll agree to abide by her recommendation. How's that?"

Knowing it was probably the best concession he would get from her, he agreed. "What time is your mom coming to watch Abby?"

"2:00," she said, "so I had better get a move on. Can you take Abby and lay her on the bed? Hopefully, she'll sleep a little longer and I can get ready."

"I'm ready," said Josiah. "Unless you need my help with something, I can sit here with Abby."

Knowing Abby was more likely to stay asleep in her daddy's arms than on the bed and that if she could sleep a longer her mood would be better for her grandma, she agreed. Josiah helped her to her feet and carefully took Abby. As he was sitting down her eyes fluttered open for a moment, she gave a hint of a smile then closing her eyes and cuddling up to her daddy she slipped back to sleep. As Josiah watched his child sleep, he praised God for this beautiful child. The world may view her as damaged or imperfect, but in the eyes of her daddy, she was his little princess and couldn't be more perfect.

As Kate went into the bedroom to get ready, she thought about Joe's concern about her going to the doctor's appointment tomorrow. They had seen this specialist several times and liked his bedside manner and respected and trusted his knowledge concerning their daughter's hearing loss. That was why they were willing to make the two-and-a-half-hour drive, each way, to see him. Added to the drive was the fact that his office was in a huge medical center. It often took them 10 minutes to park and another 15-20 minutes to get up to his office and signed in. If they could get in and out of the office in an hour, they were looking at close to a 7-hour trip and that didn't count stopping to eat! She knew Joe was right and she would be exhausted by the time they got home. She loved him even more for his concern and care for her, but she also knew how hard a trip that long with Abby would be with only one adult. Abby was beginning to communicate in signs and would get upset when she wasn't understood. Her determination to communicate had caused her to progress further and faster than her speech and language therapist had expected. They also spoke as they signed in hopes that one day, she would also learn to read lips and speak to enable her to communicate with people who didn't sign. However, to communicate with her you had to be looking at her and have both hands free. That was an impossibility when you were driving. For Joe to go alone would be very stressful on both. And besides, she was anxious to hear the doctor's report and wanted to be with Joe when he received it. And to miss being there when Abby first got her hearing aids was not something she wanted to even consider. Both Kate and Joe wanted a big family- Kate teased about having a dozen. As much as they loved Abby, they weren't sure they would go ahead with their plans if the results of the tests indicated the likelihood that further children would also be deaf. Having finished her shower and slipped into a yellow and white sundress that was still comfortable with her increasing size, she turned on the radio to the local Christian station. As the music played softly, she prayed that with her hearing aids Abby would be able to hear the music. As she brushed her hair, she debated whether to leave it down even though the day was warm. She could ask Joe to turn on the air conditioner in the car so the wind from an open window wouldn't blow her hair into a tangled mess. It would be easier to pull it back, but the seat in the car hit it just right to prevent her from sitting comfortably. And she would have to lay on her back for the ultrasound. That position was uncomfortable enough this late in the pregnancy without having her hair up. She decided to leave it down. Her hair done, Kate opened the closet and took out a pair of white sandals with heels. She loved heels and these were a gift from Joe. She smiled as she thought about Joe's gift. Joe had gotten them for her on Mother's Day. At 5'3" she wasn't overly short but compared to Joe's 6'4" frame she felt tiny. When they were dating and first married. she often wore heels to reduce the difference. When Abby started walking, she quit buying heels. Without being able to call Abby away from danger, she needed to always be able to move quickly and her daughter's safety was more important than heels. Joe had given them to her for Mother's Day saying they were for the rare times when they went out without Abby. Due to her special needs, they didn't like to leave her with anyone other than their family. They thanked God that their parents both lived local, as did their siblings, and that they all loved spending time with Abby. As she slipped her feet into the sandals she glanced at the clock and saw that it was 1:48. Her mom, Ruth Landers, was usually early unlike Kate who usually ran about 5 minutes late. Today she was ready on time. Would she have to wait for her mom? She couldn't remember ever having to wait for her mom. It had been her mom encouraging her to hurry since she was a little girl. As she reached for her purse, she heard her mother come in the front door and smiled. No, she wouldn't have to wait. True to form her mother was early. She left the bedroom to go greet her mom.

2

When Kate entered the living room, she saw Abby still cuddled in her daddy's arms. Her blue eyes were open, but she was not fully awake yet. Kate always felt a catch in her throat when she saw their small daughter in her daddy's arms. Abby was petite but Joe's size dwarfed her even more. Her love for this child had grown during the months she had carried her before she was born, and her diagnosis of deafness didn't even dent the depth of her love. Abby's deafness had been discovered just hours after her birth when Joe met his daughter for the first time. And yet he loved her unconditionally. The child she carried gave a swift kick and stirred Kate into motion. She moved toward Joe and Abby and as soon as she had Abby's attention she signed and spoke "let's go potty." Abby lifted her arms to her mother. Kate wasn't sure if Abby understood what she had signed, knew the after-nap routine, or simply desired to be held by her mother. Whatever the reason, Kate picked up her daughter and proceeded into the bathroom. With their mission accomplished and the sticker applied to the potty chart, Kate and Abby went into the kitchen where Joe had set out Abby's snack. Slipping her into her chair Kate signed and spoke

"Mommy and daddy are going to the doctor's. You stay with grandma, and we will be home for supper."

She must have understood some of it because she looked at grandma and waved goodbye to Joe and Kate. Kate turned to Ruth and said,

"We should be back by 4:30 but if not, would you put the casserole from the refrigerator into the oven?"

"Not a problem," answered her mom.

Kate and Joe each kissed Abby who was so busy with her fish crackers she hardly noticed and headed for the door. Outside Kate inhaled deeply. There were several large lilac bushes near their door and Kate loved the fragrance. The day was pleasantly warm with just a slight breeze, and she almost wished they were just going for a walk and not to an appointment. Almost. But they hoped that today they would find out if this new baby was Grace or Daniel. They had had a previous ultrasound, but the technician had not been able to get a definitive view. They didn't care but because they had known that Abby was a girl months before her birth all their baby clothes were pink and purple. She smiled at the thought of Daniel being dressed in a little pink dress with lace trim. Joe caught her smile and offered a penny for her thoughts.

"I was just picturing Daniel in a pink lace dress," she said.

He gave a mock growl and said, "not my son."

"Well, if we find out it's a boy how about we stop at the mall after tomorrow's appointment and pick up something blue?"

Joe responded, "about that, I'm still not sure you should be going."

"I know and I appreciate your concern, but I think I'll be fine. Still, I agreed to heed the doctor's recommendation."

He kissed her forehead lightly as he helped her into the car and went around to his side and got in. After buckling his seatbelt, he turned to her and said, "you do know I want you there with me, don't you?"

"Yes," she answered. "If the news is not what we are hoping for, I wouldn't want to hear it alone.

"Exactly, but if it's good news I want to be able to share that with you too. It's just I am concerned about you and this new little one and that outweighs my need to have you right there. We started with finding out if Abby's deafness was genetic or simply a gift of God before we knew this baby was on the way. Who would have known it would take this long to get answers. We would have known 2 months ago, but we had to cancel that appointment because Abby had a stomach bug. And the doctor didn't have any openings until tomorrow."

"Sure, he did," Kate teased. "At 8:00 in the morning."

Joe smiled and teased back "and who didn't want to leave the house at 5:00 am miss I'm not a morning person?"

Kate laughed and responded, "guilty as charged."

Joe was a morning person and was eager to rise and start each day. Abby was just like her daddy and early mornings often found the two of them sharing breakfast before Kate struggled to rise at 6:30. The baby kicked at that moment reminding Kate that God was going to bless them again soon and she sighed contentedly. She closed her eyes and as she relaxed and enjoyed the wonder of her baby's movements, she recalled what Joe had said a few minutes before when he referred to Abby's deafness as a gift of God. Opening her eyes, she turned to Joe and asked,

"What did you mean about Abby's deafness being a gift from God?"

He grinned and responded "I wondered if you caught that. I've been praying about Abby's deafness and about the possibility that the new baby will also be deaf. Specifically, I've been praying about my attitude. Two weeks ago, when I picked Abby up from nursery after church another dad was there at the same time. When his daughter spotted him, she ran towards him calling daddy, daddy. When Abby spotted me, she ran toward me with a grin on her face and jumped into my arms. At that moment it hit me I may never hear my child call me daddy with the unconditional love I heard in that other little girl's voice. And it saddened me, and I prayed fervently for 2 days that this new baby would be perfect. Then God spoke to me asking if I believed that Abby was a gift from him. Of course, I believed that. Aren't my gifts good and perfect? Well, I knew that *verse,* and realization dawned on me. If I believe God's gifts are good and perfect, and that Abby is a gift from God, then Abby and her deafness must be a gift from God. Do I still desire to hear my child call me daddy? Of course, but if it never happens, I trust God that his plan is perfect."

With tears in her eyes, Kate thanked her husband for his words. She too had struggled with not being called mama and it helped to know Joe felt it too. She then spent the rest of the drive thanking God for his gifts specifically Joe, Abby, and their new little one.

As Joe pulled into a parking space at the hospital where the ultrasound was to be performed, she added to her prayer if it is your will God, could we please find out if we are having a girl or a boy? Oh, and let the doctor say I can go to the appointment tomorrow. Amen.

Joe finished parking the car and came around to help

Kate out of the car. As they made their way inside, they held hands and remained silent both occupied with thoughts about the ultrasound that would hopefully reveal that all was well with their child. And maybe let them know if they needed to shop for blue clothes. Before Abby, Joe would have said he wanted a son, but another princess-like Abby would be great too. Kate on the other hand wanted to give Joe a son. What man didn't want a son? But if she was honest with herself, she was kind of hoping this baby was another girl. Two girls close in age to share a room, secrets and of course, all of Abby's newborn clothes would work for this one too. Since they hoped for more babies, Joe could have a son later. She must have giggled because Joe raised an eyebrow at her as he held the door open for her to enter.

Kate grinned and said, "I was just trying to rationalize whether we should have a boy or a girl and then realized how silly that was. The baby is already a girl or a boy and nothing will change that."

He tried not to laugh, but when she grinned at herself, he broke into laughter, and she joined him.

Soon Kate was up on the examining table, Joe right beside her waiting for the technician to start the ultrasound. As the technician squirted the gel on her belly, she asked,

"Do you know what you are having?"

"No," they answered together.

"Do you want to know," she asked.

"Definitely," Joe answered.

The technician looked at Kate. "And you want to know, too?"

Kate gave an enthusiastic "yes.'

"Ok," the technician said with a smile," let's see if this

little one will cooperate." Less than a minute later, the technician pointed to a place on the screen and said, "See that, it's a little girl."

"Hi Gracie," Kate said softly, but not so softly the technician didn't hear.

"Grace what?" she asked.

"Grace Joy," answered Joe.

"That's pretty," the technician said.

Twenty minutes later, Kate was dressed again, and they were heading for her doctor's appointment across the street. They had a little time, so they walked slowly each thinking about the news that they were soon to have another little girl.

It wasn't long before Kate was seated on another examining table this time waiting for the doctor. They only had to wait a few minutes before Dr. Sylvan arrived. She had delivered Abby and they both trusted her completely. After examining Kate and assuring them that the ultrasound and her exam both indicated that everything was great, she asked the couple if they had any questions. They looked at each other and Joe gave Kate a look that told her he wanted her to present the question to Dr. Sylvan. Kate took a deep breath and explained about the appointment the next day telling her that they expected to learn if Abby's deafness was genetic or not. She explained that although they really wanted to be together to hear the news, Joe could call her from the hospital or even have her on speakerphone when he met with the doctor. But also, Abby was getting her hearing aids and Kate wanted to be there. She was completely honest about the length of the day, the distance they had to travel, and the birthday picnic the following day. Dr. Sylvan thought for a moment and had a couple of questions for her.

"How involved are you in the preparations for and the running of the birthday party?"

"My preparations are all done and once we get there, Joe's sister, Karen, is in charge."

"Can Joe drop you at the door and then take Abby with him to park?"

She glanced at Joe who responded, "sure."

"Do you have cell phones?"

"Yes."

She turned to Kate and asked, "have you been having any contractions?"

"Just an occasional Braxton Hicks."

"How occasional? Dr. Sylvan asked.

"Once or twice a day," Kate responded.

"That's normal and they will probably increase in frequency as you get closer to your due date. Since you were late with Abby and you show no sign of going into labor in the next couple of weeks, I don't see any reason you shouldn't go, if you promise to take your time walking and remember to take along plenty of water. And promise to let Joe carry that precious little Abby. While she is little, let her big, tall daddy do the carrying." The doctor turned to Joe and asked if he was comfortable with that? Seeing he wasn't convinced; she added, "the trip shouldn't trigger labor even if Kate gets tired. She might not be as comfortable physically as she would at home, but she will be emotionally more comfortable with you, and I think that is more important. Besides even if she goes into labor, you'll be together and at a hospital. And since the hospital you are delivering at is a half-hour closer to the appointment than your house, you will never be more than an hour from a hospital. Rarely does a woman deliver within an hour of her first contraction. The ultrasound indicated that even if the baby was born tomorrow, she is fully developed, and while she only weighs about 5 pounds right now. she should do just fine. I see no reason why Kate shouldn't go."

At that Joe's face relaxed and he said, "ok, we agreed to abide by your recommendation. And it is easier to travel with Abby with two people."

"Ok, I'll see you in two weeks, if there are no more questions." She looked from one to the other and seeing them both shake their heads, she went out the door.

As they walked back to the car Kate asked Joe, "are you really ok with me going tomorrow?"

He thought for a minute and said "yes."

"Thank you," she responded and took his hand.

He bent down and placed a kiss on the top of her head and said, "I love you."

"I love you too."

Joe helped her into the car and got in. "Windows or air conditioning?" he asked.

She thought for a minute before answering "windows" knowing her husband preferred the fresh air to the a/c. They both rolled down their window and let the early summer breeze blow their hair. Kate soon grabbed a hair tie and pulled her hair into a ponytail on the side of her head. Now the wind wouldn't blow it and it wouldn't be uncomfortable against the seat. She'd pull it out as soon as she got home. She didn't need to look in a mirror to know exactly how it looked. At this time of day, the Christian radio station was playing praise and worship music. Both

Joe and Kate rode in silence for the first ten minutes each caught up in their own thoughts. After ten minutes first Joe, then Kate began to sing quietly with the radio. By the time they arrived home, they were both singing loudly praising and worshipping God in song.

3

Kate groaned as her alarm went off. It took her a minute to figure out why it was going off so early. When she remembered, she smiled. Today was Abby's birthday and it was hearing aid day. Kate pushed the thought of the test results from her mind. Until she heard the results, she could tell herself that Abby's deafness was not genetic and there was no chance baby Grace, or any future babies would also be deaf. She could hear Joe in the kitchen working with Abby on her morning word. They had set a goal to teach Abby at least two new words each day. Mornings were for nouns. They had a box of 3x5 cards with pictures on them. Abby would pick one from the new pile and one she already knew. First Joe would quiz her to see if she remembered the old one. She almost always did. Then he would teach her the new one. They would spend time playing a game where they would take turns signing the two words. Later in the day, they would work on verbs. Kate decided she had better get moving if they were going to get everything done before they had to leave for Abby's appointment. She quickly dressed, picked up Abby's gifts, and headed to the kitchen. She smiled as she heard Joe and Abby going over Abby's words. Abby had picked dog again. She picked it so often they were tempted to hide it. One of her presents was a stuffed dog that did flips when it heard a noise. Abby's speech therapist had recommended it to encourage Abby to start vocalizing sounds. They all hoped that someday Abby would have at least some ability to speak, especially now with her getting hearing aids. Kate paused in the kitchen doorway, watching her family. When Abby spotted her in the doorway, she stared with big round eyes at the gifts Kate carried. Kate set them on the table in front of her daughter. After signing and singing Happy Birthday, they encouraged her to open the gifts. As expected, the dog was a favorite. The new sundress and barrettes just weren't as exciting as the dog. They showed her how to make it flip by clapping her hands. Joe lifted Abby and her dog to the floor so she could play with it for a few minutes, while Kate went for a cup of coffee. Joe reached for their Bible and read Psalm 139. When he got to verse 13, he paused and looked at Kate. With tears sparkling in her eyes, they quoted the next verses together from memory.

For you created my inmost being, you knit me together in my mother's womb.

I praise you because I am fearfully and wonderfully made. Your works are wonderful, I know that full well.

After they finished reading, they joined hands and prayed. When they finished Joe picked up Abby and her new sundress and went to get her ready to go. Kate refilled her coffee cup, popped a bagel in the toaster, and pulled the crockpot out of the refrigerator. Setting it on the counter she plugged it in. She had assembled crockpot macaroni and cheese last night. It was Abby's favorite and would be all ready for the birthday supper when they got home. Thirty minutes later they were out the door. Joe had loaded the diaper bag with extra clothes, snacks, sippy cups, and lunch into the car while Kate had been brushing Abby's hair. He still wasn't sure that Kate should go, but he figured she could rest in the car. He put two water bottles in the cup holders in the front of the car. Abby's car seat had a cup holder and he put her sippy cup in there. He made sure she had toys where she could reach them and went back in to see if they were ready. He found mother and daughter waiting right inside the door both looking ready for summer in their sundresses and sandals. Abby had the new dog clutched in her arms. He looked to his wife and asked, "the dog is going?"

"Yes, she was insistent and kept signing dog, car, bye-bye. It was such a good use of her signs I couldn't turn her down".

"Ok then, let's go" and he scooped up small child and stuffed dog in one arm and held the door for his wife with the other. The ride to the doctor's was uneventful. Abby played with her new dog most of the way. Their appointment was scheduled for 11:30, right when Abby usually ate lunch, so they had timed their arrival to allow them to eat some lunch before going into the hospital where the doctor's office was located. Kate was happy to see that they had managed to get all of Abby's lunch in her and not on her or her parents either.

When they were finally in the examining room waiting for the doctor, they began to get a little nervous. Abby was sitting on the floor playing with her dog. Seeing Kate fidgeting, Joe took her hand and prayed, "Father calm us down and help us to trust you in this and all things. Amen."

Just as he finished the doctor entered the room. He took time to interact with Abby first, signing and speaking to her about her dog. Then he sat and faced Kate and Joe. "I have the results of the tests and there is good news and bad news. The good news is that we have identified the cause of Abby's deafness and there are no other abnormalities associated with it. The bad news is that it is a genetic condition and any other children you choose to have may also have hearing loss. However, the loss may not be as severe as Abby's. This condition can range from mild to profound hearing loss. Only about 5% of the children affected have a hearing loss as severe as Abby". He asked if they had any questions. They didn't currently. "Call me if you think of some," he encouraged. "When is this little one due?" he asked.

"She's due to arrive in about 5 ½ weeks," Kate answered.

"I'd like to see her in September, if that's alright with you, especially if she passes the newborn hearing test." Seeing their confused looks he explained, "If she fails, you will know she has a hearing loss and use all you've learned with Abby to give her the best treatment possible. What we are finding with this condition is that about 10% of the children pass the hearing test because the loss is mild. The parents don't realize their child has a problem until they fail to start talking and by the time the child receives a diagnosis and help, they are 3 or 4 years old and have fallen behind their peers."

"We will make an appointment for Grace for September," said Joe.

"Ok," said the doctor. "We have gotten that covered.

Now let's get to the important part of the day." He picked up the phone and said just two words, "we're ready."

In just a minute the door opened and in walked the speech pathologist, Carla. She bent down and signed "hi" to Abby.

Abby signed "hi" and then signed, "hi dog."

Carla smiled and signed "hi" to dog. Then she signed "come" and held out her hand to Abby.

Abby signed, "dog."

Carla said and signed, "yes, dog can come too." Carla led Abby over to the examining table and Joe boosted her up onto the table. Carla fitted the hearing aids into Abby's ears. Abby touched them but didn't seem bothered by them. Carla smiled and signed, "good. Ok," she said. "Is everyone ready for me to turn them on?"

Joe and Kate said, "yes," almost in a whisper. Carla switched them on and nodded to Joe and Kate to say something. Kate called Abby's name softly signing at the same time. Abby's eyes got big as she looked at her mom.

Joe said and signed, "I love you, Abby." Abby's eyes moved to Joe's face. She definitely heard them!

Carla explained it would take her time to recognize words and sounds. She suggested that for the time being, they continue to sign and speak.

Joe and Kate were overwhelmed with emotion. Their precious Abby could hear them. And maybe one day soon she would speak. Joe and Kate thanked the doctor and Carla and prepared to leave. Joe signed, "time to leave." Abby put her hands over her hearing aids and shook her head, no.

Kate immediately understood Abby thought the hearing aids were like the toys at the doctor's office. She thought they had to stay at the office. She gently touched the hearing aids and signed, "these are Abby's."

She knew Abby understood, because she immediately touched them and signed, "go, Abby, dog?" When they reassured her that the hearing aids were indeed going, she jumped up and waved goodbye to Carla and the doctor.

4

Kate sat on the bench in front of the hospital waiting for Josiah to pull the car around from the parking garage. She was glad for a moment alone to think about what the doctor had said. Just as Joe and Abby disappeared, Kate felt a contraction. It didn't last long and while she felt it, it wasn't bad. A Braxton Hicks she concluded. "Good thing daddy wasn't here for that," she told Grace. "He would have worried for sure." Love for her family brought a lump to her throat. She leaned back and relaxed knowing that by the time Joe buckled Abby into her car seat, paid for parking, and got around to this side of the hospital fifteen to twenty minutes would have passed. The sun was shining and while the day was warm, it was pleasantly so. Even the news that Abby's deafness was genetic and each child they were to have would be at risk for the same didn't get her down on this beautiful day. Especially in light that Abby's case was the severest possible. No other abnormalities related to the condition and many children only suffered a mild to moderate hearing loss. Grace could have perfect hearing, a mild loss, or she could be like Abby and profoundly deaf. But she wasn't at risk for further complications. They knew deafness and were not frightened by it. When a second contraction seized her just seven minutes after the first Kate was a little concerned. She had never had two Braxton Hicks so close together. She prayed, "Lord, do I tell Joe?" She didn't think it was really labor, and she didn't want to deliver this far from home. Her mom was supposed to take Abby, and she wanted Dr. Sylvan to deliver her baby. She would not tell Joe. He had a two-and-a-half-hour drive and didn't need to be worrying about her. Six minutes later she had a third contraction a little longer and harder than the first two. Still, she reasoned I was in labor for seventeen hours with Abby. If this is labor, I have plenty of time. She shifted her position. Six minutes came and went. No contraction. Seven minutes no contraction. She saw Joe pull into the circle in front of the hospital to pick her up. She could see Abby almost asleep in her car seat. It was way past her naptime. If I have a contraction while getting in the car, Joe's sure to notice she thought. She got in the car and buckled up without any more contractions. She glanced at Abby and saw she was asleep as Joe pulled away from the curb and began the trip home. As Joe pulled onto the entrance ramp for the highway, she glanced at the clock. Fourteen minutes-no contraction.

"Why don't you nap for a while," Joe suggested. "I'll wake you if Abby wakes."

"Ok," Kate responded and reclined her seat. She was just drifting off when another contraction hit. It was longer and stronger than any Braxton Hicks she had ever experienced. It was strong enough that for the first time she began to rethink her decision not to tell Joe. Over the next forty-five minutes, she had five more contractions at irregular intervals. A glance at Joe let her know he wasn't aware yet of what was happening. She didn't dare glance into the backseat to see if Abby was still asleep for fear of alerting Joe to what was happening. She was beginning to wonder if she was really in labor. She knew that in another fifteen minutes they would be halfway and was sure she could convince Joe to continue towards home. As another contraction gripped her, she wondered if she could continue to hide them. When another one hit only four minutes later, she wondered if she should hide them. After three more contractions, each only four minutes apart, she decided she was really in labor and needed to tell Joe. And call her mom to meet them at the hospital!

"Joe, would you take the exit for the hospital? I'm going to call my mom and ask her to meet us there."

"Why? What? What's happening?" Joe sputtered, his face paling considerably.

"I've been having some contractions. At first, I thought they were Braxton Hicks, so I didn't say anything. I didn't want you to worry. But they've been getting stronger and more regular, and I think we had better stop at the hospital." She got quiet for a minute and then reached for her phone.

As she was dialing, he said not asked, "you just had one didn't you."

She had just confirmed it when her mother answered. Her mom asked exactly where they were and quickly agreed to meet her at the emergency room door in 40 minutes. She had just hung up when another contraction came.

When he saw her relax, Joe said, "that was only four minutes. How long have they been that close?"

"Just the last five or six I think."

"Call the doctor quick before you have another one.

Tell her we are on the way and ask her if she thinks it is safe to keep driving."

She started to laugh and ask what else were they going to do when another contraction hit. As soon as it subsided, she called the doctor. The line was busy. Twenty minutes and six contractions later she finally reached the doctor.

"Has your water broken was her first question?"

"No."

"Good, keep coming. I'll warn the emergency room to meet you at the door. What about Abby?" she wanted to know.

"My mom is meeting us there to take Abby."

"I think you still have plenty of time but let's get you inside and checked out as quickly as possible. And be sure your seat is reclined."

"Don't worry," Kate said, "it is. Joe says will be there in fifteen minutes." As soon as she hung up the strongest contraction yet hit. Just as it ended her phone rang. It was Dr. Sylvan.

"As a precaution, I've asked the police to meet you on the exit ramp. The car will be pulled on the shoulder. Pull up behind it and flash your lights twice and they'll get you here without slowing down for lights."

"Ok." She waited out another contraction and then told Joe what Dr. Sylvan had said. She had just finished telling Joe when they got to the exit ramp and there was the police car waiting with flashing lights. Joe flashed his lights twice and the officer immediately turned on the siren and headed for the hospital. They both were relieved that the police had wasted no time in getting started.

When the latest contraction ended, Kate said, "that was a bad one."

"Hold on," Joe begged her, "we'll be there in five minutes or less."

She didn't respond and Joe glanced over at her to see she was having another contraction. With the police escort, they were at the hospital in four minutes and Kate had had two more contractions. As the pulled into the emergency room at the hospital she was relieved to see Dr. Sylvan and a stretcher. She didn't think she could sit in a wheelchair, and she was sure she'd never make it to the maternity ward on foot. As soon as the car was stopped the nurses had the door open but had to wait until the next contraction subsided to get Kate out of the car. Just as they got her on the stretcher Ruth ran up. "Give me the keys," she said, "and go."

Joe tossed her the keys calling as he ran, "park and bring Abby up. I don't think it will be long." And with that, he was in the hospital racing down the hall after his wife's stretcher. Kate was taken right into the delivery room where a nurse was waiting.

"My name is Amy. Has your water broken?" Kate who couldn't answer because she was in the middle of a contraction started to shake her head no when she felt a rush of warm water. "I see," said Amy, "well, let's get you out of that dress, cleaned up, and into bed. Then Dr. Sylvan will be in to see you."

Kate just managed to say "no time" before another contraction started. Amy had been a delivery room nurse for fifteen years and had learned to listen to the women she helped. Grabbing a pair of scissors, she quickly pulled up Kate's dress and proceeded to cut off her panties. As soon as the panties were out of the way Amy saw a head of dark hair.

Pushing the call button, she said "we need Dr. Sylvan and dad STAT." With the next contraction, Grace Joy Kanell entered the world protesting loudly just as her daddy and doctor reached the doorway. Amy had the baby's mouth suctioned and had her wrapped in a blanket by the time the doctor got her gloves on. As Dr. Sylvan finished with Kate, Grace got to meet her mommy and daddy. They were allowed to spend about ten minutes with their new daughter before the neonatologist arrived.

"Congratulations on your new daughter," he said after he had introduced himself. "I don't think anything is wrong but because she is over a month early, I would like to take your daughter to the Neonatal Intensive Care Unit also known as the NICU for evaluation. Get settled in your room and I will be in to see you in about a half-hour." They reluctantly surrendered their daughter, just as Ruth arrived at the door.

Joe said, "Look quick, grandma, there goes Grace." The doctor kindly stopped and let Ruth get a quick peek before heading to the NICU.

"Where's Abby? Kate asked.

"Entertaining the nurses at the nurses' station, I'll go get her as soon as you tell me where Grace is going and why."

"They are taking her to the NICU for evaluation just as a precaution," answered Joe.

Amy who had been on the phone came over then and said "we are all set. Let's head up to room 321." Having heard Ruth say that Abby was at the nurses' station, she said, "We go right by there and you can grab her on the way." And with that, they were off.

Thirty-five minutes later Kate was settled in her room and beginning to wonder about Grace. She was relieved when there was a knock on the door and the neonatologist entered carrying Grace. Joe who didn't like the look on the doctor's face took his daughter and went over to stand by the bed. Her eyes were on the baby, and she didn't seem to notice the doctor's expression. He cleared his throat and began, "her lungs are good and almost everything checked out perfectly."

"Almost?" asked Joe.

"She failed her hearing test, didn't she?" said Kate.

"Yes, but how did you know?" asked the doctor. "Our daughter Abby is profoundly deaf. We found out this morning that the cause of her deafness is genetic and that there was a probability that other of our children may also be deaf."

"Just because she failed the test doesn't mean she is profoundly deaf," the doctor explained.

"We know and she already has an appointment with a specialist," responded Kate.

"Well, if you don't have any questions, I have sick babies to see. I'll let your family get acquainted with this little beauty." As he left, Ruth lifted Abby onto the bed to meet her new sister.

5

Kate woke slowly the next morning disoriented by unfamiliar sounds. As she became aware of where she was, she smiled and rolled on her side. In the bassinet next to her hospital bed was Grace Joy sleeping peacefully. They had had a good night. She had been up to nurse at 2 am. Then, as previously agreed on, she went to the NICU to be monitored until her 5 am feeding. The doctors had found nothing wrong. They claimed the only sign that she had been born over a month early was her size. At four pounds thirteen ounces they didn't expect her to have any difficulties but as a precaution, they wanted to keep a close eye on her for a couple of days. Kate knew they wanted to keep her until at least Sunday, maybe Monday. They wanted to be sure she was nursing well and didn't develop jaundice. Kate was anxious to be home, but for her daughter's health, she would follow the doctor's recommendation. She glanced at the clock and saw that it was 7:30 am. Should she chance showering now, hoping Grace stayed asleep, or wait until she fed her again? Well, she could get her stuff around for her shower and then decide. Maybe she'd call Joe and try to catch him before he left the house to drop Abby at his mom's for the morning. Nana and Papa would bring her by after her nap and meet their newest granddaughter then. Her parents had both been here last night. She hadn't known it when they first got to the hospital, but her dad had spotted their car at the emergency room door and dropped her mom off, and then went to park. Everything had gone so fast once they reached the hospital, there had been no time to talk until later. "You were in a mighty big hurry little girl," she whispered to her daughter. She slowly sat up and was surprised at how good she felt. Moving carefully, she stood and headed to the bathroom. As she came out her mom entered her hospital room.

After a quick hug, her mom said "if you want to shower, I'll keep an eye on Grace. I talked to Joe about seven and he said he was headed to his mom's and should be here a little after eight."

That decided it for Kate. She would shower now and leave Grace in her grandma's very capable hands. The warm water felt good, and Kate took her time knowing that once she was home taking a long shower would be a rare treat. By the time she turned off the water, she could hear her mom talking to Grace. She could picture the two of them. Her mom would be holding the baby out in front of her so she could talk right to her face. She was probably standing and swaying slightly. She loved the fact that their extended family had always talked to Abby even with the knowledge of her hearing loss. And that the whole family was learning to sign.

Her brother had summed it up nicely, "if that's the language Abby will use, then we had better know it too."

Having slipped on her new peach nightgown and matching robe, she slid her feet into her slippers, and grabbing her hairbrush she left the bathroom. She smiled as she saw she had been right about how her mom was holding Grace. She'd been wrong, however, about her mom standing. She was sitting in the rocking chair. "Has she been up long?"

"Only about 3 minutes."

"Just let me brush my hair and I'll take her."

"No hurry, we are just fine."

As Kate brushed her hair, her mom commented that it was nice that she had the room to herself. "They aren't going to put anyone in here with us because they want Grace to be protected from germs that visitors might bring in."

"That makes sense. Are they allowing you visitors?" questioned Ruth.

"Family only and Abby is the only child allowed in. Joe asked his mom to spread the news to his family. The church sent out a notice about Grace's birth and included no visitors allowed. The only problem is Grace may miss out on meeting her future husband."

Ruth laughed. "That did work out pretty well, didn't it?"

By the time Kate finished brushing her hair, Grace was ready to eat. Kate took her daughter, quickly changed her diaper, and then settled into the other rocking chair. One of the perks of having a double room to herself was two rocking chairs. She had just gotten Grace to start eating when Joe arrived. He carried a single rosebud in one hand and a bagel in the other. He had brought her the same two items when Abby was born. Abby's pink rosebud was pressed in her baby book. Grace's was a cream-colored rose with pink edges. The bagel was because he knew that was how she preferred to start her day. Not being a morning person, she didn't like to decide what to eat that early. So, she just had the same thing almost every morning, a bagel. And a cup of tea. But he knew she could get that from the hospital. Or he could. Seeing her occupied, he looked around the room for a cup of tea. He didn't see any but asked her anyway if she wanted a cup of tea.

"Yes, please, that would be nice."

"I'll be right back."

"Joe," he turned around, "you won't disturb her." Joe grinned and came towards Kate. He too had wanted a kiss, but he didn't want to disturb the baby. He gave her a lingering kiss and then straightened up to go and get her cup of tea. She heard his phone start to ring as the door closed. She then raised the baby to her shoulder and patted her back. She was rewarded with a good burp. After resettling her daughter so she could finish eating, "she asked what's happening with the picnic?"

"Everyone decided to wait until you and Grace can come."

"Sounds like a good plan." Kate was pleased. She would never have asked them to postpone the picnic, but she would have hated to miss it. By the time Joe returned with her cup of tea, Grace was done eating and Ruth had left to run some errands. Joe set the tea on the table next to Kate and reached for the baby. Cuddling her close he settled himself in the other rocking chair.

"My mom called."

"I heard you talking to her as you left," said Kate.

"My mom says Abby is helping her in the garden. They are planting squash this morning. She figured Abby would do better with something with bigger seeds. She was very impressed. She showed Abby just once to put two seeds in each hole and Abby followed along and put two seeds in each hole her nana made. She said, she'll take Abby over to our house in a little while and wash up the box of baby clothes that I took out of the attic after the ultrasound on Thursday. Was that just thirty-six hours ago? So much has happened."

"Yes, miss Grace was in a bit of a hurry. But you know what this means don't you?"

"No, what?"

"She will be a month and a half when the youth retreat starts. You'll be able to go! Isn't God good?"

"I hadn't thought of that. Are you sure you'll be alright? We can see how the next week or so goes before we decide for sure."

"We'll be fine. Both our moms are ready and willing to help. You've been working on your lesson material for months. Go, teach, have fun."

"I love you. Thanks."

"Love you too," said Kate.

He laid the sleeping baby back in the bassinet and pulled Kate into his arms for a kiss. Just then there was a knock on the door. Joe called come in and their pediatrician, Dr. Lowe, stuck her head in the door. "I heard someone was in a bit of a hurry last night," she said.

"Someone was in a very big hurry last night," Joe said with a laugh.

Dr. Lowe joined in the laughter and then said, "I'm going over to the NICU to check on all the reports and then I'll be back to see your little one."

Joe suggested they have their devotions while they waited and pulled out his pocket Bible. Opening to Psalm 139 he began to read. They had just finished praying together when Dr. Lowe returned. After she had finished examining Grace, she handed her to Kate. She pulled over one of the room's straight chairs and sat down. "Have a seat and let's talk," she told them. They sat down nervously.

"Everything looks good," she said. "Except for failing her newborn hearing test, there is nothing wrong with her. When she was in the NICU being monitored, all her readings were completely normal. However, due to her size and the fact she was in a hurry and didn't get that last month, I want to take some precautions. She is so small that an infection could be serious. So, until she is seven pounds, no going out in public. Only family holds her and by family, I mean your immediate family, your parents, and your siblings. I know you want to take her out to church and everyone will want to see the baby. I'm recommending you wait. I am asking you to wait the four to six weeks it should take her to get to seven pounds. She was down a half-ounce this morning. It's perfectly normal for a baby to drop a little weight right after birth. If she's back up to her birth weight tomorrow, you can go home late in the afternoon. Otherwise, I'd like her to stay until Monday. All this hinges on her continuing to do good. If anything develops- and I don't anticipate it- we will readdress your discharge time. Any questions?" They both shook their heads no. As she headed out the door she turned and said, "Oh and I'll want to see her in my office on Tuesday morning for a weight check. Remember to use the side door for healthy infants, not the main waiting room."

6

Tuesday night shortly after 8 pm, Kate had just finished feeding the baby and tucked her into her crib. She poured two glasses of iced tea and sat down on the couch to wait for Joe. She only had to wait about five minutes before he came down the hall with a sigh. "Abby is finally asleep."

"Grace is too."

"Abby didn't want to close her eyes tonight. I think she was afraid you would leave again. She would start to settle and then sit up and sign Mommy go. I reassured her at least ten times that mommy wasn't going anywhere tonight. She finally settled. Have you been waiting long?"

"Only about five minutes." There was a cd of praise and worship music playing softly. Joe came and sat on the couch, reaching for his glass of iced tea.

"Thanks, that's good, iced tea."

"Your mom made it before she left. Mine is never quite as good as hers." This was the first time they had been home and alone together in days. Kate and Grace had come home Monday afternoon. Joe's mom and dad had been there to help with Abby until late last night. Kate's mom and dad came first thing this morning to watch Abby, while they took Grace in for her weight check. The doctor had been pleased that her weight was up to five lbs. Now all grandparents had gone home. Because the doctor had again stressed the need to protect Grace from illness until she reached seven lbs. the rest of their extended family decided to delay coming to see the new baby. The birthday picnic was tentatively rescheduled for the middle of August in hopes that Grace would be up to the required weight by then. Also, Joe's sister was getting married at the end of June and after a honeymoon, Karen and Eric were going on a two-week missionary trip. Kate cuddled up next to Joe and for a while, they just sat there enjoying being together without company. After twenty minutes or so Kate spoke up. "It's amazing how God worked things out, isn't it? Not sure what she was referring to, Joe asked her to explain what she meant. "Things in general, the safe arrival of Grace and how well she's doing but specifically the teen retreat. Grace will be six weeks by the time you go. By then we will be in a routine. Our moms will both be available if I need help. You can go and enjoy your time without worrying about us. I probably won't be able to join you as I have in the past. I doubt Grace will be big enough to be in public yet and I won't be able to leave her. If I had gone into labor while you were at camp and delivered that quickly you might have missed the birth."

"I was with you throughout labor and almost missed it as it was," he said with a grin. "She certainly was in a hurry, wasn't she? For a while, I wasn't sure we would make it to the hospital."

"I'm really glad we did."

"Me, too!" said Joe.

She was so quiet after that he wondered if she had fallen

asleep. He was just about to say something when she spoke again. "What are we going to do about what the doctor said?"

He suspected she was referring to the diagnosis of Abby's and now Grace's deafness as genetic. He had hoped they wouldn't need to discuss that until Grace saw the specialist in September. In case she was talking about something else, anything else, he asked her to explain.

"About more children. We want a big family, but what if they are all deaf? Would God do that to us? If we had more children with hearing losses, it could interfere with you serving as a youth minister. We hope that Abby will speak one day, especially with her hearing aids. And we don't know about Grace."

He could tell she was getting very emotional. He pulled her close and said, "God knows what we can handle, and he knows our desire for a big family. You're tired and emotional right now. We need to have this discussion and we will, but let's wait until I get back from the teen retreat. We'll get my mom to stay with at least Abby and we will go for a drive and get some ice cream and talk. How does that sound?"

She thought for a moment. She knew he was right. Her emotions were in no shape for a discussion that was sure to be emotional. She didn't want to wait but could see the wisdom in his suggestion. Finally, she said "ok" and could feel him relax. "Do I have to wait until after the teen retreat to get ice cream?"

He laughed and said, "not if we have some."

"Your mom dropped off mint chocolate chip and caramel praline turtle today."

"Two dishes of mint chocolate chip ice cream coming

up," he teased knowing that while it was his favorite, she'd rather go without than eat the mint ice cream.

"Are you really hungry" she teased back? "What about me?"

"I'll share," he said and headed for the kitchen. He was soon back with two dishes of ice cream – one of each flavor. After finishing their ice cream, they each picked up a book and settled in on the couch to read. It wasn't long before Joe noticed that Kate had fallen asleep. He gently took her book and she slid down into a more comfortable position. He debated waking her to go to bed. A quick glance at the clock told him Grace would be up for a feeding in about forty-five minutes. If he woke her, she'd get changed into her pajamas, brush her teeth, and any number of little things until the baby woke. If she got that all done now, she could go to sleep as soon as she was done feeding Grace. But if he woke her and Grace slept longer than usual, she'd be sitting around waiting. He decided to let her sleep. Forty-four minutes later, as if she had an alarm, he could hear Grace stirring. He gently woke his wife and when she sat up, he stood up and went to pick up his daughter. He gently laid her on the changing table and began to change her diaper. He talked to her softly, even with the realization that she couldn't hear him, and her eyes weren't able to focus enough to begin learning lip reading. He knew that some of the newborn hearing tests were inaccurate. A little boy at church had failed the hearing test and later testing revealed his hearing was fine. Just in case, they were going to talk to Grace. As he finished zipping up her pink and purple flowered sleeper, he heard Kate come in the room behind him. He picked up

Grace and cuddled her close as he turned around to Kate. "All clean and ready to eat."

"Thanks, and for letting me sleep. Sorry I was such poor company. Our first evening together in a while and what do I do? Fall asleep!"

"I understand you are tired. It's not a problem for me. You need to sleep when you can for the next few months until Grace starts sleeping through the night. Remember Dr. Lowe said she may need a night feeding longer than Abby did because she is so much smaller."

"Thanks for understanding," Kate said as she reached for her daughter. Kate started talking softly to Grace as she headed to the rocking chair.

Yes, they would talk to Grace in case the test was wrong. But in his heart, Joe knew that the test was accurate. He knew that like her big sister Grace was deaf. And he felt a peace from God about it. The question of whether to have more children, he wasn't ready for that one yet. He was glad Kate had agreed to wait until after the teen retreat to discuss it. He honestly believed she needed more time before she was ready to deal with the emotional issue. But to be honest she wasn't the only one who needed time. He was fairly certain they would decide not to have more children and he wasn't ready to let their dream of a big family die just yet.

JULY 18TH

Kate was running behind. Joe had left for the teen retreat yesterday. She knew it was going to be a long week but was glad he had gone. She wasn't sure he would until he actually got in the car and backed out the driveway. Her mom would be here any minute to watch Abby while she took Grace to her checkup. There Grace was ready. Again. She had spit up on her first outfit and had to be dressed again. Kate had been on time until then. She smiled at her small daughter and laid her on the bed. She was such a good baby. Abby was playing on the floor with her doll mimicking what Kate did with Grace. Kate checked the clock and sighed. She needed to be out the door in five minutes. Abby was still in her pajamas, and she still needed to do her hair and teeth. She had packed the diaper bag last night so at least that was ready. She heard her mom come in the front door and called out that she was in the bedroom. She quickly picked up her hairbrush and ran it through her hair. Setting the hairbrush down she deftly did a French braid and turned as she heard her mom enter the bedroom. "Would you mind getting Abby dressed? Her clothes are

44

on her bed. Grace spit up and had to be changed and now I'm running behind."

"Of course, I'll dress Abby. It's no problem at all. Do you think you'll be home for lunch?" Ruth asked as Kate hurried into the adjoining bathroom to brush her teeth. Ruth waited correctly assuming that Kate had heard and would answer once she got her mouth emptied of toothpaste.

"My appointment is at 9:00 so I don't see any reason not to be back." She came out of the bathroom to find that Ruth had buckled the baby into her infant car seat. "Thanks, mom."

"You're welcome, it gave me a reason to pick up my youngest granddaughter and cuddle her a minute."

"Like you need a reason to pick up either of your granddaughters," she teased. They laughed as Kate began to gather her purse, and the diaper bag made sure she had a pacifier and reached for her daughter's car seat.

"Your dad suggested you three come join us for lunch. We can pick up take out on the way."

Kate thought about what she had to do and how hard it was to get out of the house. While the baby had been gaining steadily, she had not made it to seven pounds yet. Kate couldn't even go to church. At her two-week, checkup the doctor had okayed them to go to their parents with her if none of the rest of the extended family was there. "I'd love to," said Kate, "but now I need to get out of here." She got Abby's attention and told her bye she'd see her later and hurried out the door.

At the doctor's office, the nurses all fussed over tiny Grace. With lots of hair, dark like her daddy, and those big bright eyes she was a beauty. When Dr. Lowe came in, she exclaimed over the barrette that held Grace's hair out of her face. As she made eye contact with the baby, she commented, "she is unusually alert for a one-month-old baby let alone one who had been born a month early. Did the nurse weigh her yet?"

"No, she was just about to when another nurse stuck her head in the door saying she needed help in a room down the hall."

"Well let's see how big you are." Kate laid the baby on the scale and was thrilled to see the scale register seven lbs. three oz.

"Way to go, Grace," she exclaimed happily.

After the doctor had checked her over and declared her to be in great shape, she turned to Kate and seeing the hopeful look on her face as she finished dressing Grace, laughed. "Yes, you can go out in public but limit who can hold her. I know everyone and their cousin will want to see and hold the beautiful new baby. Give her another month. Family only. You can go to church, but no church nursery or small crowded rooms. I'd still suggest you avoid the grocery store unless you keep her in her car seat with a blanket over it to keep strangers from cooing over her and breathing germs on her. Any questions?"

"Yes. Joe is at a youth retreat. Can I go up and spend a couple of days with him?"

The doctor thought for a minute. "Will you and Joe have a room separate from all the others?"

"Yes, there is a small cabin for the director that he uses."

"Then I don't see any reason why you can't spend the rest of the week as long as you and Joe are the only ones to hold her."

"Great," she said eagerly buckling her daughter into the

car seat and gathering her stuff to leave. As she went out into the sunny day she was rejoicing, feeling like she had been given her freedom. Grace still nursed every two to three hours, so she hadn't been able to go much of anywhere the last month. With the precautionary restrictions on taking Grace out, she had begun to get cabin fever. And she could surprise Joe at the teen retreat! She was glad the radio was playing some familiar songs and sang along as she drove home.

She couldn't keep her happiness from showing as she entered the apartment. Her mom smiled at her and said, "I take it she's doing well?"

"She weighed seven lbs. three oz and we can go out in public with some restrictions."

"Did you ask if you can go see Joe?"

"Dr. Lowe said we can go as long as we don't let anyone else hold her and avoid small, crowded rooms."

"Well let's get everyone packed. Abby can stay with us, and you can head out to the camp."

"Are you sure? I could take her with me."

"We've been wanting an excuse for her to spend the night, and this is it. I'll bring her up to camp tomorrow afternoon."

Kate checked the time. "If we hurry and leave now, we can get to camp before Grace needs to be fed. I can have lunch with Joe. You and dad can enjoy lunch with Abby." And with that Ruth went to pack a bag for Abby and Kate went to get her things and the baby's ready. By 10:30 they were on their way. Kate and Grace headed to camp and Joe. Abby and Grandma heading to surprise grandpa.

Joe left the dining hall at about eleven. After breakfast, he had met with all the staff to go over the plans for the rest of today and tomorrow. He glanced at the road that led into camp. Spotting what looked like their minivan coming down the road he started to panic. He checked his phone- no missed calls. He looked down the road again. It was definitely their car. He realized that if there was a problem at home, Kate would have called not come looking for him. She was close enough now that he could see her face. She was smiling so all was well. She spotted him then and her smile broadened. He could see Grace's car seat but not Abby's. He jogged over to the car as Kate pulled into a parking space. Kate was soon out of the car and in his arms. After exchanging a kiss, he pulled back and said, "It's not that I'm complaining but what's going on?"

"Grace had her check-up this morning and she weighed seven pounds three ounces. Dr. Lowe said we could spend the rest of the week as long as we avoid small-crowded areas and no one else holds her."

"Terrific! Where's Abby?"

"My mom wanted to have her spend the night. She will bring her up to camp tomorrow."

"I've got about a half-hour free right now before I lead chapel, let's take your things to the cabin." He opened the trunk and took out Grace's stroller. Kate unhooked the infant seat from the car and hooked it into the stroller while Joe grabbed their bags. She was grateful that the stroller had a net that would keep people from reaching right into the stroller. She joyfully followed Joe up the path that led to the director's cabin. She knew from the past that it was a small two-room cabin. There was a small bedroom with a queen-size bed and a combination kitchenette living room. By the time they put up a cot for Abby and the pack and play for Grace, the room would be snug. She didn't care at all. She was with Joe.

Once things were settled in the cabin, Joe headed to the chapel. Kate headed to the camp kitchen. Joe had suggested that she head that way. He had told her that Jenny who was serving as camp cook seemed to be understandably overwhelmed. Kate knew that Jenny had experience working as a cook at a local college. Jenny and her husband, Nathan, had recently moved to the area and started attending their church. They had a three-year-old son named Samuel. Kate hadn't met her because she hadn't been to church since Grace was born. As Kate entered the dining hall and headed toward the kitchen, she was surprised to hear crying. It sounded like a newborn and a baby were both crying. Kate pushed open the swinging door and just stood there staring. There was a newborn crying. A little boy who looked to be about a year old was sitting in a pack and play crying. And a young woman, who Kate assumed was Jenny had tears running down her cheeks.

"Hi, I'm Kate Kanell. Are you Jenny?" Jenny sniffed and nodded yes. "Joe sent me to see if I can help. I'm a little confused. I thought you had a three-year-old son?"

Jenny answered, "we do. He's with Nate."

"So, who are these two?"

"Foster children that were placed with us yesterday. The timing wasn't great but when we found out they will probably be available for adoption, we couldn't say no. But I can't get them to drink anything. Jackson is 13 months and has eaten but won't drink anything. Not as worried about him. I have been able to get him to eat and he loves jello. Right now, he's tired. If I could get Andy to settle, I think Jackson would fall asleep. Any advice or help would be appreciated. If Andy doesn't start drinking by 1 this afternoon the social worker is going to pick up both boys and take them to the hospital. I don't know if we will get them back."

"Oh no," said Kate. "We have got to figure this out. First Jackson. Have you tried a bottle? Sippy cup?"

"A bottle and three different sippy cups- hard spout, soft spout, and straw. Nothing worked."

"How about no spout," asked Kate? Seeing Jenny's puzzled expression, she reached in her diaper bag and pulled out Abby's sippy without a spout. "Here try this," Jenny added milk and offered it to Jackson who reached for it and immediately began to drink. "One down one to go. Has Andy's mom been able to tell you what kind of bottle she used?"

"His parents are both dead."

"Oh, that's terrible," said Kate. "Do you have any idea what she was like?"

Jenny responded, "the social worker thought she was a good mom. The kids were clean and well-dressed. Their car seats are nice and in great condition. Everything points to them being well cared for."

Kate thought about this and questioned, "I wonder if she was breastfeeding him? Maybe he's never had a bottle. How desperate are you?"

Jenny looked at Kate and answered, "very."

"Desperate enough to let me try to nurse him?"

Jenny looked at her with understanding dawning on her. "I'm willing to give it a try but what about your own little one?"

Kate laughed and said, "no worries I could easily

feed triplets!" With that, Kate picked up baby Andy who immediately began to root. Kate walked over to a chair in the corner and prepared to feed the baby. As soon as he was in position, he began to eat hungrily. "Mystery solved. We will figure this out," Kate assured Jenny. As Andy continued to nurse, they both noticed that Jackson had fallen asleep.

Jenny whispered, "I best get working on lunch." By the time the teens arrived for lunch, it was ready. Andy had finished eating and was asleep. Grace had been fed and was back to sleep. Jackson was still asleep.

When chapel started at seven that evening, Kate had fed both Andy and Grace. Grace wasn't quite asleep, but her eyelids were fluttering. Nate and Jenny had taken their three little ones to their cabin to try and get them settled and into bed. The previous night had been rough and none of them had gotten much sleep. Nate was reluctant to go feeling, that he should be available to help Joe. Nate and Joe had developed a deep friendship in the weeks leading up to camp as they prayed and planned together for the retreat. Joe assured him he had enough help and that tonight Nate's priority needed to be his family. Jenny and Kate had agreed that Jenny would bring Andy over to Kate's cabin at ten. Kate would keep him and nurse him through the night. Tomorrow they would begin the process of getting him to accept a bottle. Kate slipped into the back of the chapel just as the first song ended. Joe stepped up to the microphone. After leading the teens in prayer, Joe made a few announcements about evening activities. After chapel, there would be free time until nine when they would gather for testimonies and singing around the campfire. Lights out would be at eleven that evening. Now," said Joe, "I have a special announcement. All of you know our daughter Grace was born prematurely. I thank you for your prayers. You also know that the doctor wanted Grace to weigh seven pounds before we took her out in public. This morning Kate took Grace to the doctor, and she weighed seven pounds three ounces." At that, the entire chapel erupted in clapping, cheers, and loud whistles. Grace had been almost asleep and startled awake at the noise. Kate was surprised. It was the first time Grace had responded to noise. Kate tried not to get too hopeful, telling herself it was very loud and the whole room seemed to vibrate. Joe let them go for a minute because in truth he felt like joining them. After a minute he held up his hand for silence. He didn't think that the kids had spotted Kate and Grace in the back yet. When the kids were quiet, Joe continued, "Grace is allowed to be out in public, but her immune system is still immature. I have to ask you to keep your distance for a little while yet. Please do not get close or try to touch her yet. In case you haven't noticed, Kate and Grace are here tonight. Abby is with her grandma but will be up tomorrow after she has speech therapy. I am thankful for the way you all interact with Abby, and she loves your attention. Please keep in mind that Abby is only two and doesn't understand protecting Grace. She just loves her little sister. If you aren't feeling well, please keep your distance from Abby. If Abby gets sick, she will expose Grace. And keep praying. Someone may ask don't you trust God to protect Grace? And the answer is absolutely. But I also believe God expects us to use our heads and do our part. I wouldn't get in a car without brakes and pray ok God, I know this car doesn't have brakes, so I am trusting you to get me safely to my destination. Could God do it? Absolutely! But should I do it? No! Luke 4:12 says *"Jesus answered, It is said; do not put the Lord your God to the test."*

"I don't believe many people would test God by driving around without any brakes. Or jump out of an airplane without a parachute. Personally," said Joe, "I wouldn't jump out of a plane with a parachute." A teen boy called out coward and a ripple of laughter spread through the chapel. Good thought Joe I have their attention. "I do think that many people put God to the test regarding heaven and what happens after we die. Especially young people. Many, young people believe that Jesus died on the cross. They believe he died and rose again. They believe heaven is real. But it is just a head knowledge. James 2:19 says,

"you believe that there is one God, Good! Even the demons believe that – and shudder."

"Many people believe a loving God will not send people to hell. I agree a loving God will not send people to hell. But he loves us enough to let us choose hell. You see young people the choice is ours. We can choose heaven by following God's way or WE can choose hell. God doesn't send us to hell. He lets us choose. Just like he doesn't send us to hell, neither does he send us to heaven. The choice is ours. The other way we test God is by assuming we are going to live to be old. We believe that we need to decide to follow Jesus, but we realize that following Jesus requires a commitment and we want to wait until we are older. A popular attitude is you are only young once. I'll do what I want now and accept Jesus when I'm thirty or forty or seventy. We test God to let us live that long. You have gotten to know Nate and Jenny over the last month. They have given me permission to share it with you. When their son Sammy was born, neither Nate nor Jenny were Christians.

Neither one had grown up attending church and knew very little about God. The birth was very hard, and Jenny almost died. She was in a coma for two weeks. Her recovery was long and hard. The doctor warned Nate that if Jenny survived and was to get pregnant again, she likely wouldn't survive next time. They wanted a large family. While Jenny was still in the coma, Nate made sure Jenny would never get pregnant again. When Jenny came out of the coma, she was very upset and almost left Nate. Instead, they attended counseling with a pastor and accepted Christ. They still want more children, so they have become foster parents and hope to adopt. Many of you have met Jackson and Andrew. The boys are currently their foster children, but they hope to be able to adopt both boys. I praise God for giving them another opportunity. No one is guaranteed to live another day. Don't put off accepting Christ's invitation. If you have never made a decision for Christ, I urge you to really think about it. It's something that shouldn't be made lightly. It's the biggest decision of your life. We will be talking about it all week. I pray that if you have questions you will talk to someone tonight. There will be people here in the chapel during free time tonight who will be happy to talk to you. Please don't put off this decision."

Throughout the rest of the week, the two women worked together to get Andy to accept a bottle. Each day after lunch Kate and Jenny would settle the kids for a nap and spend time sharing with each other about their past and their hopes for the future. Samuel had become Abby's best friend and watched out for her as only a three-year-old could. By the time the retreat was over Kate and Jenny had each declared that the other was the sister they had always longed for.

8

After breakfast on Saturday Jenny and Kate prepared to head home. Nate and Joe would stick around until about four. On the last day, the teens always did a service project for the camp as a thank you for the use of the camp. Since the camp staff returned today, they didn't have access to the kitchen. Joe always ordered pizza for lunch. This year's project was to paint the outside of the craft building.

Nate and Jenny only had one vehicle. Since Nate and Joe both needed their cars to give teens a ride back to church, Kate and Jenny decided to take the five kids and head home in Kate's minivan. They were barely off the camp property before all five children were sound asleep. With Christian music playing quietly in the background, the two mothers returned to their favorite topic of conversation- children and everything children. They had talked all week and not exhausted that topic of conversation! Jenny had shared how angry she was when she found out she would never be pregnant again. At the time she felt it was worth the risk of death to have another child. Jenny was an only child and had been lonely. She had hated it. Her best friend was one of seven. No one was lonely at her house! She vowed she would have a large family. When she met Nate, she told him from the beginning that "she wanted at least six kids. He was enthusiastic about a large family." Jenny said "when he decided without even asking me, I felt betrayed. I would have taken the risk. My anger almost destroyed our marriage. In the end, as a last resort, we went to counseling with the pastor at First Community Church. He helped me see how scared Nate had been. I came to the point where I realized that Nate had been right. We couldn't risk another pregnancy and his going ahead without consulting me first was done out of fear and love. As I forgave Nate and worked at putting my marriage back together, I also realized my need for Christ. I accepted Christ a short time later. When Nate saw the difference in me, he wanted to know more. We started to attend church together and soon he accepted Christ as Lord and Savior. About a year ago our pastor was speaking on the book of James. When he got to James 1:27, it was like a light bulb exploded in my head. I turned to Nate and could tell by his expression that the verse had the same effect on him. As soon as we had lunch and got Sammy down for a nap, we memorized James 1:27."

> *Religion that God our Father accepts as pure and faultless is this: to look after orphans and widows in their distress and to keep oneself from being polluted by the world.*

Kate vaguely remembered quickly reading through that very verse just this morning. It hadn't affected her as it had obviously affected Nate and Jenny.

Jenny continued, "We both felt that God was telling us that we could still have a big family. We could adopt.

We prayed about it for a week and did some research. We found out that many of the children adopted domestically were adopted by their foster parents. The cost of foreign adoption was incredible. While we believed God could provide the funds for foreign adoption, we didn't feel him calling us to do that. We felt that God would have us foster and adopt domestically. We went through the classes and got certified as foster parents. We owned a small three-bedroom home. We had had several short-term placements but really wanted to adopt. We found we so quickly loved the children and they felt like our own and it was hard to let them go. We also decided we wanted a bigger house. We finally found a large 6-bedroom home on 5 acres. We made an offer, and it was accepted. Our home sold within 24 hours of listing it. The only problem was it was an hour away in a different county. Nate was willing to commute but foster care is certified by counties. I contacted our caseworker who said that the two counties often worked together. We would be able to transfer everything except their worker would have to approve the new house. We didn't have any foster kids at the time so that wasn't a concern. I said goodbye and clicked off the phone. As I reached to hang it up, it rang. Caller ID identified Nate. He asked if I was sitting, and I replied should I be? He said he had just been offered a promotion that included a transfer. He would now be working 5 minutes away from the new house. So, we packed up and 2 months ago moved. When we first started looking for a new home, we hoped to be able to attend First Community Church. We had done our counseling through First Community but had been attending a small church near our old home. This county decided to redo all the clearances before certifying us to foster. They must be redone every year and we were due to have them redone 3 months after moving so it made sense. It also gave us time to settle in. We had also stressed to our new worker that we were interested in adoption, and she agreed to look for children that would likely be available for adoption eventually. When I heard the announcement 3 weeks ago that a cook was needed for the teen retreat, I knew I could do it. Our clearances weren't back yet so we had no extra kids. So, I volunteered. Our clearances came through last week. Sunday morning, we got a call. They had two babies needing a home. The dad had killed the mom, then turned the gun on himself. No extended family is willing to take the kids so they were most likely going to be freed. Could we take them? I said I needed to check with Nate and would get back to her within the hour. I said I was sure Nate would agree, but that this wasn't a decision I could make on my own. She understood and said she wouldn't make any more calls until I got back to her. Nate was as thrilled as I was. He had time off from work to help here. We talked to Joe because now we would have three little ones while trying to help at camp. Joe and Nate work well together and Joe felt that Nate only being available part-time was better than no Nate. So, we came. But we wouldn't have made it without your help, Kate. I was almost ready to throw in the towel on my desire for a bigger family when you showed up on Monday."

9

They had all agreed to meet at Jenny's and Nate's place later this afternoon. Joe and Kate had decided that to them Nate and Jenny were family and Grace could be around them. On the way, they grabbed fast food for lunch knowing the kids would all wake up hungry when they pulled into the driveway. With lunch ready for the older three the moms could feed the infants. Jenny didn't give her address just told Kate when to turn.

When she pulled into Jenny's driveway, Kate couldn't believe it. "You bought the Clarks place?" she asked Jenny.

"We did. Do you know the Clarks?"

"Their daughter and I were inseparable growing up. Pointing to the large house next door," Kate asked, "have you met your neighbors yet?"

"Yes, I met Ruth and Charlie the first day we moved in. Ruth brought us a casserole and brownies for supper. Neither Nate nor I have any living relatives. Having Charlie and Ruth living next door kind of fills a gap in our lives. We've been so busy getting unpacked and recertified for foster care that we haven't had much time to get to know them. I am looking forward to spending time with Ruth and introducing our new boys to them."

"Then you don't know anything about her children?" Before Jenny could answer, Ruth came out the door and headed their way. Jenny called out a greeting and Kate said, "hi mom." At the look on Jenny's face, Kate and her mom burst out laughing.

When she had recovered from her shock, Jenny looked at Kate and asked, "your mom?" Who knows how long they might have stood there laughing if Jackson hadn't started crying? The women worked together to get the kids out of the car and into the house. With Ruth supervising the older three, Jenny and Kate were able to feed the two infants without interruption.

10

JULY 29, 2011

Josiah, Kate, and the girls had been home from camp for almost a week. Kate and Jenny had talked on the phone several times. Joe and Kate had yet to have what she liked to think of as the big discussion. Before her week at camp and her talks with Jenny, she had dreaded it. Now she was looking forward to it with at least a little bit of anticipation. She had been praying about the whole situation and was starting to wonder just what God might have in store for them. Now the time was almost on them. Joe's parents were coming in about an hour to watch Abby. Kate was putting the finishing touches on tonight's casserole for Dan, Joy, and Abby. Joe and Kate were going out for dinner. They would begin the discussion over dinner, lingering as long as Grace let them. When she started to fuss, they would walk through the park that was near the restaurant to a secluded bench to continue talking if needed. Joe had shared with his parents the topic of discussion for tonight. Dan and Joy said to take their time, they would stay as long as needed. Kate thought she had come to the point in her thinking and praying where she could take any decision as long as they decided. The casserole done, Kate popped it into the oven and went to check on Grace. She hadn't heard her yet, but Grace was such a content baby she often lay awake happily looking around for ten minutes before asking for attention. Kate was hoping Grace would wake soon so she could feed her before Joe's parents arrived. As she walked into Grace's room Kate heard Joe give Abby a five-minute warning. He had taken Abby out to the yard to play, while Kate started dinner. Kate was pleased to see Grace awake and watching her mobile. She picked the baby up smiling at her and whispering words of love. After changing her she settled into the rocking chair to feed her. She heard Joe and Abby coming in the back door. She thought again what a blessing this apartment was for now. True it was small and only had two bedrooms. The master bedroom was a decent size, but the second bedroom was small. Grace's crib and Abby's toddler bed took up most of the space. A single dresser that the girls shared, the rocking chair, and the room was slightly on the crowded side. The apartment was part of a big house that a member of their congregation had turned into three apartments. There was a wonderful fenced-in yard complete with a swing set and a sandbox and it was in a very nice neighborhood. When the church had hired Joe as their first youth pastor, the owner had come forward and offered them the apartment at a 50% discount. Since the church was prepared to pay 50% of their housing cost up to a certain amount and the offered rent was below that limit, the church board had voted unanimously to pay the entire amount. Kate raised the baby to her shoulder and was rewarded with a loud burp. Settling Grace to finish eating, Kate continued to think about the house. It didn't matter the decision that resulted from the big discussion.

At some point, they would need to think about a bigger place. Grace had finished eating and was kicking her feet and looking around from the middle of the big bed when Kate heard Joe let his parents in the door. She could hear Joy great Abby and tried to imagine what her daughter had done when she heard all three adults burst into laughter. Picking up Grace, she grabbed her purse and went out to greet her in-laws. And maybe find out what Abby was up to. When she entered the living room, she saw Abby turning somersaults. She had learned how from Sammy the previous week. "What was so funny?" Kate asked.

Dan grinned and explained that Abby had wanted papa and nana to do somersaults with her offering to teach them how. Kate understood. Abby was so thrilled with her new ability she couldn't understand why everyone else didn't want to somersault too. Joe and Dan went into the yard where Joe wanted his dad's advice on something. Joy had taken Grace in her arms, so Kate picked up Abby, and the women headed to the kitchen. Kate explained when the casserole would be done and reviewed Abby's bedtime routine. Because of the difficulty of getting Abby to sleep, Joe and Kate tried to be home by bedtime on the rare occasions they went out in the evening. With Joe's flexible schedule at the church and the fact that he worked several evenings, they were more likely to go out at lunchtime and avoid leaving Abby at bedtime. But Joe's parents both worked and Kate's parents had taken off for ten days right after the teen retreat, so if they wanted to get the big discussion done, they needed to do it in the evening. Confident that Dan and Joy could handle Abby, Kate set her on her feet and turned Abby to face her so she could tell her they were going out. She talked to her in full sentences but signed in what they considered baby talk. Her therapist had suggested this approach telling them if they used a few simple signs, Abby would pick them up faster. While she said, "Mommy and daddy are going bye-bye, you are going to stay with papa and nana, obey nana and papa and we will see you in the morning." She signed, "mommy, daddy go bye-bye, you stay nana, papa, obey, see you morning."

Abby must have understood at least part of it because she signed back, "papa go."

Kate responded, "papa here." Abby seemed to be understanding more and more of what they said to her but hadn't yet started making sounds. Joe and Dan came in at that moment, so Kate took the baby from Joy and buckled her into the car seat. Joe carried the car seat out to the car while Kate followed with the diaper bag. They made small talk in the car on the way to the restaurant. It was like they had an unspoken agreement to not start the big discussion until they were seated in the restaurant and had given their order. They were both pleased to see that Grace had fallen asleep during the ride to the restaurant. Kate pulled out a blanket from the diaper bag and covered the whole car seat to discourage eager people from getting too close to the baby. Joe had called ahead and explained the need to protect the baby from crowds and the staff had promised to save them a booth that was not in a high traffic area. They were pleased with the location of the booth they were shown. The car seat fit perfectly on the bench next to Kate and still left her with enough room to sit comfortably. Having been to this restaurant before, they both knew they wanted the fried haddock that this restaurant was famous for. Joe chose fries and Kate a baked potato. They both ordered tossed salads with house dressing. Joe ordered iced tea and Kate ordered ice water with lemon. As they sat back to wait for their salads and drinks Joe suggested they pray. He could see Kate was impatient to start the discussion, and if he was honest with himself so was he. As Joe finished praying including what they were going to discuss as well as the meal, he saw the waitress coming with their salads. As soon as she left Joe looked at Kate, then down at his salad and said, "I don't think we should have any more children. I've prayed and prayed, and I don't feel a peace about bringing another baby into this world knowing that it will likely have a hearing disability. I know how much we both wanted a big family, but I feel this is best." He hadn't been able to look Kate in the eyes while he was speaking afraid if he saw what he expected in her eyes, he would back down and not say it. When he finally looked into her eyes, he saw sadness but also acceptance.

"I agree," she said. "I didn't want to at first, but I've been praying too. God has given me a peace that we shouldn't try to conceive another child. However, he has also opened my eyes to the possibility of adding to our family by adoption."

As the idea began to take route in Joe's mind a smile spread across his face. "I don't know why I didn't think of it, the amount of time we've spent with Jenny, Nate, and their three." All through their salads, their fish, and cups of coffee they discussed the possibility. They discussed domestic vs. international. Both felt that God's plan for them at this time was domestic. International would involve travel and with Abby and Grace, they were not comfortable with traveling outside the US at this time. There were a few negatives they discussed. Things like the fact that the likelihood of them getting a domestic infant to adopt was slim because they had biological children.

Kate looked at Grace and with tears in her eyes said, "I dearly love babies and I'll admit the idea of never having another infant to cuddle and nurse saddens me. However, I trust God to know best. If it is his plan for me to have another infant, we will have one. If it isn't part of his perfect plan, why would I want to go against his plan?"

Joe looked into his wife's eyes and said, "I love you."

She responded, "I love you too." They sat just looking into each other's eyes without speaking for several minutes until Grace began to stir. Checking the time and realizing that Grace had given them twenty minutes longer than normal, they decided they had better get a move on before Grace made her presence known. As they sat on the park bench while Kate fed Grace, they talked about adoption versus foster care. As they walked through the park, they discussed boys versus girls. As they drove home, they discussed ages and how many.

As they pulled into the driveway, Joe turned to Kate and said, "let's not tell anyone in our families yet. Let's talk to Jenny and Nate and get some more details. Let's talk to an agency. When we know more, then we can tell them. OK?"

"I think that's a great idea," she said.

Joe's parents had known what they were planning on discussing. He saw his mom's questioning look and just said, "the discussion went very well. We just need to get a little more information before we make a final decision. We'll let you know as soon as we are sure what we are doing."

"Ok," Joy answered with a sigh. "Abby was an angel

and went to sleep without too much trouble. Your casserole was delicious by the way. Can I have the recipe?"

"Sure, I got it online, so I'll email you a copy." Joe and Kate thanked them again and Joy and Dan headed out the door. Joe went to check on Abby and Kate laid the sleeping Grace in her crib. She hoped Grace would sleep about another hour. If she had her final feeding close to 10 pm she would usually sleep until 3 am and then go back out until 7 am. That was a schedule Kate could handle without too much trouble.

When Joe came back into the living room after checking on Abby, he sat down on the couch and looked at Kate. "There is one question we haven't touched on all evening."

"Are you referring to how we prevent future pregnancies? I've been thinking about that. Would you be devastated if I did get pregnant?"

"No, I just don't think it's wise," said Joe

"I agree totally. I don't want to do a permanent surgical procedure for either of us. I think I'd like to talk to Dr. Sylvan and find a method of birth control that has very high accuracy. If God chooses to send us a baby even with good birth control, he will give us the strength to parent that child deaf or hearing."

"I never thought of it that way, but I couldn't agree more." They both felt the need to unwind and let the discussion rest before bed. They did agree that Kate would call Jenny in the morning and invite them over for dinner soon. They also agreed to hire a couple of teens to keep an eye on the kids and give the parents time to talk. They rejected playing a board game afraid they would continue to talk. Instead, Joe popped in a movie, and they sat together. It took some time for either of them to pull in their thoughts and pay attention to the movie, but by 10:15 when Grace woke for her feeding, they were both enjoying the movie. The movie ended just as Grace finished, so Kate changed her and tucked her into bed. Joe was sitting on the side of the bed looking thoughtful when Kate came into the bedroom. He looked up and said, "do you think we could start with one or two? I don't think I could handle four more at once."

Kate laughed and said, "I agree with one or two to start unless of course, God has other plans." Kate and Joe prayed together and climbed into bed.

Kate was almost asleep when Joe said, "we need a bigger house."

11

Kate called Jenny the next morning. Jenny had known that the big discussion was taking place the night before. She had been ready to call them last night and find out their decision, but Nate had suggested that they pray for them instead. Jenny hadn't wanted to admit it, but she knew Nate was right. When all the kids were asleep for the night, the couple who understood so well the decision facing their friends petitioned their Heavenly Father to give Kate and Joe wisdom and peace.

When Jenny answered the phone on the first ring, Kate had to laugh. "Were you waiting for me to call or something?"

Jenny laughed too. "I wanted to call last night but Nate suggested we pray instead. We prayed, but I wasn't going to give you much longer before I called you. Fourteen minutes to be exact!"

"What do you mean?"

"I told myself I would give you until 9:00 to call. That's in fourteen minutes.

"And then, what?"

"I was calling you." The women shared a laugh before Jenny demanded, "so did you talk?"

"We did."

"And?"

"It went well."

"Kate! Are you going to tell me? Don't keep me in suspense!"

"I called to invite you, Nate, and the kids to dinner at your earliest convenience.?

"What?"

"Come to dinner, soon. We want to talk to you guys. We'll tell you about what happened."

"Have you been reading Esther?"

Kate laughed catching her friend's reference to Queen Esther who invited the king to dine with her before she made her request. They tentatively planned for that very evening each needing to check with their husbands. Neither one wanted to wait any longer than necessary.

"Are you sure you want us to bring the kids? It's easier to talk without the kids running around. We don't mind getting a sitter".

"We enjoy the kids and besides Joe suggested we get a sitter or two here to watch the kids. Abby loves your kids, and the interaction is so good for her."

"What should I bring?"

"How about a dessert? I think we'll throw burgers on the grill, and I'll make a potato salad."

"Sounds good, I'll get back to you after I check with Nate. And don't even think of pulling an Esther and making us wait until the next night's dinner."

"I won't, I'm just bursting to tell you." And both hung up the phone still chuckling.

That evening when Nate and his family pulled into the driveway at the Kanells,' Abby was on the swing set.

Two teen girls that Jenny recognized from the retreat were playing with her. Sammy saw Abby right away and begged to go play with her. He had assumed the job of Abby's friend, teacher, and protector. He wanted every story signed, so he could learn words for Abby. He loved to walk around the house and ask signs for whatever he saw. To his credit, he was picking up signs at an amazing rate. Jenny had asked Kate how come he could learn them so fast when Abby had to work at learning them? Kate had explained it was because he already had a language and was just learning a new one. Abby was learning her first language. Sammy knows what a dog is. He understands that it has a name. Now you are giving him an additional name for dog. Abby is still learning that the sign for dog is the name of that kind of animal. That made sense to Jenny.

As soon as he was released from his car seat, and out of the van he went tearing through the gate and right up to Abby. He went right in front of her and as soon as she looked at him, he signed, "hi Abby."

She signed, "hi Sam."

Jenny unbuckled Jackson while Nate lifted Andy and his car seat out. Jenny swung him on her hip and grabbed the diaper bag. Nate grabbed a container of chocolate chip cookies and three half gallons of ice cream. Jenny had had the kids all ready when Nate got home from work at 3:30 so they arrived at the Kanell's a little before 4. Jenny and Kate had wanted to have time to talk before supper. They were afraid if they didn't, it would be bedtime before they got done. And there certainly wasn't room to sleep all 5 kids in Joe's and Kate's apartment. As she walked across the yard Jenny noticed the teen girls seemed to be doing well the kids. One of the girls offered to watch Andy in the playpen if she wanted. Seeing her hesitation, the teen pointed out the video monitor set up on the picnic table. Pastor Joe said that the kids play nice together, but he was going to keep an eye on things from inside. He told us not to come in because he felt it was too many kids for one person. If we need anything we just have to call out, and he will hear. Jenny glanced at the sleeping baby in the car seat and said they would take him with them. Seeing the disappointed look on the young girl's face she added that if he woke up, she'd bring him out.

When Jenny went into the apartment, she was surprised to find the others waiting for her in the dining room. "Have we gone formal today?" she joked.

"No," answered Kate. "The kitchen windows are open. Since you will be the first to know what we decided we don't want the teen girls to hear it and accidentally spill the news to our families."

Joe added, "with the monitor, we can be in here, so we won't be overheard and still keep an eye on the backyard."

"I never would have thought of the monitor," said Nate.

"Alright already," said Jenny with a laugh, "we can discuss baby monitors later. I want to hear about the big discussion."

The others joined in the laughter and Joe said, "let's start with prayer." He thanked God for friends and their time together. He prayed for God's leading in their lives. As soon as he said amen, he nodded to Kate who looked ready to burst.

With tears in her eyes, she turned to Jenny and Nate. "Because of you two the hardest decision we have ever had to make has gone from being devastating to joyful. We have decided not to have any more biological children.

We are not going to undergo a surgical procedure because we would not be devastated if God in his wisdom sends us a child despite precautions. We are going to adopt. We do want more children and after praying and talking we both feel peace about our decision." Kate and Jenny were immediately in each other's arms hugging and crying and talking at the same time. The men leaned back in their chairs and grinned at their wives.

Nate said, "the funny thing is they will both be able to tell us what the other said."

Eventually, the women calmed down enough for the couples to talk about the steps involved. Joe said, "we would like to get started in the process soon, but we know would have to find a bigger place first."

"Not necessarily," said Nate. "You will need to take ten weeks of classes to start the process. After the classes, it can take a month or more to get to the point where you are ready to have them check your house. These classes are typically only offered twice a year. You then have a full year to finish your home study. There is a class starting in September. The next one probably won't be until April. If you think you will be ready to start looking before a year from now, I'd suggest you take the classes in September. They are designed to give you a clear picture of what to expect. They will help you decide if you want to foster, adopt, or are open to both. We personally found it very hard to watch the kids go back home. We have decided we want to adopt only but will take at-risk placements."

"At-risk?" questioned Joe.

Nate explained, "an at-risk placement is kids that are being placed in the hopes we can adopt them, but parental rights have not been completely terminated yet. Like

Jackson and Andy. Their caseworker has filed the papers in court to free them for adoption. But until the judge signs them, there is no guarantee. If you choose to adopt only it may be a year or more before a child is available. It will depend on a lot of factors."

"Like what?" asked Kate.

"How old a child you will accept is a big factor. If you will take a sibling group or a child with a disability, it could be less." Just then they heard Andy begin to fuss and realized they needed to get supper on the table. The two couples working together soon had supper ready and with the help of the two teens, the children were fed and happily out in the yard an hour later. They had used paper plates,clean up was easy. In record time the parents had joined the kids in the yard. Each couple paid one of the sitters and Joe drove them home. The adults knew they would discuss adoption more in the days and weeks ahead. For now, though they were going to enjoy the kids God had already sent their way.

12

Kate's parents got home Wednesday morning. They had had a great time but were anxious to catch up with their kids and grandkids. As soon as they finished unpacking, they called and invited everyone over for dinner on Sunday after church including as usual Dan, Joy, Karen, and Eric.

"Perfect," said Kate, "we have news to share and a question that needs to be answered by the whole family." Joe and Kate felt like Sunday would never arrive. They had talked and prayed about an idea they wanted to share with the family. They prayed that if the family didn't agree, God would give them peace. They wanted everyone to be ok with it but knew they might not. After all, the rest of the family didn't know Jenny and Nate, as well as Joe and Kate did.

Before Sunday arrived, there was Bible study to look forward to. Kate and Joe and their siblings usually got together on Friday evenings for dinner, Bible study, and games. They would meet at Zeke's house, and each brings part of the meal. They had not met together since before Grace's birth. Zach and his wife Lydia had welcomed their son Mark on June 19th. Zeke and his wife Leah had welcomed their son Luke on June 23rd. And Karen and Eric got married in June, went on a short honeymoon, and then went on a mission trip to distribute wheelchairs in a third-world country. Kate and Joe hadn't seen them to hear about their mission trip yet, so they were looking forward to that. Kate had asked everyone if she could invite Jenny and Nate and received a unanimous yes. She had not told Jenny that her brothers were identical twins. She also hadn't told her that they were married to identical twins. She didn't think Joe had told Nate either. Since she had told her brothers, who loved to joke around, that at least Jenny didn't know about the two sets of identical twins, she figured they were in for a good laugh!

On Friday night Kate was packing up the brownies, ice cream, and chocolate syrup for their dessert as Joe was putting Grace in her car seat. She wanted to be sure she was there before Jenny and Nate so she could see their reaction to her brothers and their wives. The evening was scheduled to start at 5:00. Joe and Kate arrived at 4:45 to find her brothers both dressed in navy shorts and matching light blue tee shirts. Kate knew immediately that they had done it on purpose and had something planned. Kate took the brownies into the kitchen to find Lydia and Leah dressed in matching white shorts and pink tops. This is going to be fun she thought as she greeted her sisters-in-law. "Are the babies dressed identically too?" she asked.

"But of course," answered Lydia with a laugh. Just then Zach came into the kitchen and said that Nate, Jenny, and their kids had just pulled into the driveway. Leah picked up Luke and went to greet her guests. Joe was on hand to make introductions. Kate heard Jenny ask where she should put the salad that she had brought. Leah said to take it right into the kitchen and she followed as did Zeke.

Joe motioned to Nate that they should follow too. Leah was keeping up a conversation with Jenny as they entered the kitchen. When she came face to face with Zach and Lydia, Jenny screamed and almost tossed the salad. Nate peered into the kitchen to see what had caused his wife to scream. When he saw Zach, Lydia, and the baby he burst out laughing. Everyone soon joined in.

Nate said, "I want to hear this story."

"It's a good one," said Joe.

Eric and Karen arrived then asked why the two couples were dressed identical and the laughter started again.

Over dinner, the two sets of twins shared their story. During their first semester in college Zach and Lydia had been assigned to work on a project together for their communications class. Zach had a book in his dorm room that he thought would be helpful for Lydia's part of the project. They agreed to meet in the campus center at 5:30. Lydia arrived before Zach, but at the same time as Zeke. When she approached Zeke, he didn't have a clue what was going on. He apologized and said he didn't have a book for her and said he wasn't even in communications class. Lydia was totally confused and headed back to her dorm. As she left Zach came into the campus center. Looking around for Lydia, he spotted Leah and tried to give her the book. She assured him she didn't know who he was and that she wasn't even in a communications class. Later that evening when Zach and Zeke talked about what had happened, Zeke suggested the possibility that Lydia had a twin. Zach responded could be and suggested Zeke go with him to communications class tomorrow morning. Zeke agreed readily. Meanwhile, across campus Leah and Lydia were having a similar conversation and planning for both of them to go to communication class the next morning. The next morning Zach and Zeke arrived outside of the classroom door about ten minutes before class started. Two minutes later Lydia and Leah walked down the hall. They just stared at each other for a full minute before Zach had said "well, that explains everything." Zach and Lydia's friendship soon blossomed into love. People tried to push Zeke and Leah together, but it wasn't until the summer before their senior year that those two were willing to stop insisting they didn't care for each other. Their friendship soon grew deeper, and it wasn't long before they realized they loved each other.

After dinner, Eric and Karen began to share about their recent trip to distribute wheelchairs in a third-world country. Eric shared "a lot went on in addition to giving out the wheelchairs. We were assigned in teams. The wheelchairs had to be fitted to each person and any adjustments and modifications that were needed were done right there while the person waited. Sometimes these adjustments were minor and quickly finished. Other times they took hours. In addition to fitting the wheelchairs, the team tried to meet other needs the recipient might need. There was an older woman named Ann who had been on several trips previously. She wasn't assigned to a team but circulated throughout the room helping where needed. On the second day, our team had a little boy come to get a wheelchair. His older brother was assigned to the team next to ours. Both boys had brittle bone disease. An uncle stayed with the older boy, while the dad was with our recipient. He was ten years old, had rarely left his house, and was terrified. He had his head buried in dad's shoulder and his arms and legs wrapped around dad. There was no way this little guy was going to allow us to evaluate and fit him for a wheelchair. All our attempts only made him cling tighter. We went to Ann for advice. She had us put dad and son in a wheelchair and push both around. After a few minutes dad was able to get him to let go and turn around. Ann then brought over a pediatric wheelchair and got the brother to demonstrate climbing in and out. Next, we had dad put his younger son in the wheelchair. He was willing to sit in the chair but wasn't about to let us adjust the seat belt. We had his dad and uncle hold his hands while Ann pushed him around the room make car noises. When he seemed calm, she brought him back to our station to evaluate him and see what he needed for his own wheelchair. As we looked at him, we decided that the wheelchair he was in was perfect for him. The only adjustment it needed was to tighten the seatbelt. We talked his dad through how to adjust the seatbelt. As he left, we were praising God for the perfect chair that didn't need lengthy adjustments."

Karen said, "some of the children who came were unable to speak and had no way to communicate with their parents. Ann also taught a method of nonverbal communication to these children and their parents. A little boy and his dad came on the last day. His chair needed a lot of modifications. While we were waiting, I asked his dad if he could understand what was said to him and communicate at all. His dad said he didn't understand anything and just cried when he needed something, and they tried to guess what he needed. I started to play with him while we waited for the mechanics to work on his wheelchair. After about five minutes I put the toy into my backpack. I told him if he wanted the toy, he had to clap. I took his hands and clapped them. Immediately I returned the toy. A few minutes later I again put the toy into my backpack. He reached for it, but I reminded him to clap, and he did, I returned the toy. The third time I put it into my backpack he needed no prompting but immediately clapped. His dad was mistaken. This little boy understood! I called Ann over and she started teaching him her method of nonverbal communication. She demonstrated to both the dad and child how the system worked. She started to explain to his dad that you might have to work with your son for weeks before he understands how to use it. Even as she was explaining it to his dad the little boy started to use it to request a cracker and a drink. The dad just stood there in shock saying over and over "my son understands."

Eric continued, "The gospel was shared with every person who came as well as with all family members that accompanied them. The goal of the distribution was to provide wheelchairs to people in third-world countries that have disabilities but have no access to wheelchairs. and we did provide wheelchairs – over 200 wheelchairs in a five-day event. But so much more ministry went on in those five days."

As they finished everyone sat quietly lost in thought. After a couple of minutes, Joe said, "let's pray" and led the group in prayer.

Sunday finally arrived. Soon everyone but Karen and Eric had arrived at Ruth's and Charlie's. When they arrived 15 minutes late, Zach teased them good-naturedly saying "you are the only couple without an infant, and you are the only ones late."

Karen used to Zach and his teasing, answered back, "you just wanted me here because you knew I'd take the baby and you'd be free to watch the game on TV." Everyone laughed and Karen reached for Zach's small son, Mark.

Hearing that everyone was there, Joe came in and asked if they could have a family meeting before dinner. Ruth had known he planned on doing this, so she had made sure there was nothing that needed her attention in the kitchen. When everyone had found a seat in the spacious living room, Joe led them in prayer. When Joe said amen and opened his eyes, he found all eyes on him. "I have two things to share today," Joe started. "First after much prayer Kate and I have decided to not have any more children. As you know Abby's and now Grace's deafness are a result of a genetic abnormality. We don't feel good about bringing another child into the world who might also be deaf. However, we are praying about the possibility of adopting. We would like to ask all of you to pray with us."

Joe took a deep breath and continued, "and now we have a question to ask all of you. I think all of you have met the couple who bought Clark's place next door?" Everyone nodded yes. "Kate and Jenny have gotten very close. Nate and I have also developed a strong brotherly bond. Nate was removed from his mother's care at three and placed in foster care. At five he was placed in the permanent care of his grandparents and hasn't seen his mother since. He has no idea who his father is. His grandfather died his freshman year in high school. His grandmother died last year. His mother was an only child, so Nate has no extended family." Joe let that sink in a minute, then nodded to Kate.

"Jenny is an only child," Kate said. "She was raised by loving parents who were both only children. She knew and loved her grandparents, but they are all gone now.

Her parents were killed in a car accident when she was in college. One of the things that drew Nate and Jenny together was loneliness."

Joe took back over now. "I would like to propose to the Kanell family that we "adopt" Nate. If everyone agrees, I want us to hold a little ceremony and officially ask Nate to be part of our family. Everyone deserves to have a family." He could see his parents and sister warming to the idea.

Kate spoke up then and said, "I'd like the Landers family to do the same for Jenny."

Before anyone could say anything, Charlie said, "let's pray." He led the family in prayer. Because he didn't end in amen the others knew they could join in. As several members of the family prayed, it became obvious what the decision would be. When there was a silence not broken by anyone else praying, Dan closed their prayer time.

When everyone looked up, Dan said "I would be honored to be a father to Nate and have their children call me papa." Seeing the smiles on the faces all around him he asked, "does anyone have any doubts, questions, reasons not to do this?" No one had any objections, so he turned to Joe and Kate and asked them, "what's your plan?"

Kate said, "I'm too excited to put this off. I want to go get them right now and present our idea to them. I'm sure they will agree and then I'd like us to do a little ceremony. We wrote out a little ceremony that will just give us special memories of today." She passed out the papers and everyone caught Kate's excitement.

Ruth said, "there is plenty of food. Go get them all. Let's do this, and then celebrate with our first family dinner."

As Kate ran next door, Joe and Charlie added a leaf to the table. Lydia was waiting with the extra place settings.

When Kate and the Johnson family arrived a few minutes later, everyone was seated in the spacious living room. As Jenny and Nate took the seats obviously saved for them, seats that looked like seats of honor, they noticed the looks on everyone's faces. They had no idea what they were all up to. Dan stood up and addressed Nate. "Joe has shared with us that you don't have any extended family members. We would like to make you part of the Kanell family. Joy and I will consider you our son and Joe and Karen will consider you, their brother. We'd be honored to have you call us mom and dad if you are comfortable with it, Dan, and Joy if not. All your kids can call us Nana and Papa." Charlie jumped in before Nate could respond. "The Landers family would like to extend the same offer to Jenny except your kids will need to call us Grandma and Grandpa."

At that Jenny burst into tears and Nate took her into his arms. Joe looked at Nate and said, "I hope we haven't offended you? We just want to share our love and family with you."

Nate answered with tears running down his cheeks. "God has answered our prayers in a way we couldn't have imagined. We've seen the love showered on Abby and Grace by their grandparents and have struggled with envy. We have been praying that God would forgive us of that envy and help us to be content with all our blessings. And God answered that prayer by giving us family. And giving our children grandparents, aunts, uncles, and cousins. We are humbled and honored by your offer. We would love to be considered family!"

The room erupted in cheers. Grace snuggled up in her daddy's arms startled awake before drifting back to sleep. Joe was surprised but in the excitement that followed, forgot to mention it to Kate sure it was just a coincidence. When everyone finally settled down, first Dan then Charlie read the questions Kate had prepared. "Do you accept adoption into our family with all the rights and responsibilities of family members?"

Both Jenny and Nate responded with a very emotional, "YES!"

Then Dan turned to the assembled family. "Do you welcome Jenny and Nate into our family with full rights as family?"

With a loud yes from everyone, Dan and Charlie said, "welcome to the family."

What followed was hugs and congratulations and total chaos until Charlie let out a loud whistle. Everyone quieted down and looked at Charlie. "Our first family dinner with our new family members is ready. Joe, will you lead us in prayer?"

For the next couple of weeks, Joe and Kate continued to talk and pray about fostering, adopting, and moving. They decided they wanted to adopt not foster. Jenny had explained that when you foster a child the biological parents are usually still involved. The biological parents would probably have weekly visits, sometimes as many as three or more each week. The children could stay for a few days, weeks, or even months. As foster parents, Joe and Kate were likely to be asked to supervise visits between the children and the biological parents in their home with Abby and Grace there. Jenny said they could request that the visits take place somewhere else with the county providing a worker to supervise. Because of the needs of Abby and Grace, their request would probably be approved. While Joe and Kate could see the great possibility for touching the lives of the parents, they had concluded that they were unable to deal with the disruption foster care would cause to their family at this time. They were also concerned that with Abby's and Grace's communication difficulties they would not be able to explain foster kids coming and going. They didn't want to risk either of the girls being afraid they would sometime leave as the foster kids did. They were not saying they would never be foster parents, but for now, they would only take children for adoption. They also prayed about at-risk placements. They finally decided they would accept an at-risk placement if there was no visitation between the child and the biological family. They finally reached all these conclusions on the third Friday in August. They decided they would take the weekend without talking about adoption. They would spend time with just the girls enjoying being a family. On Monday morning, if they still felt strongly that God's plan for them was adoption, they would call and enroll in the adoption classes. And start to look for a house. The church had been willing to pay the entire rent on their apartment because the church member had offered them such a generous deal. They were skeptical they would find another such deal but trusted God to lead them. They hoped to find a five- or six-bedroom home so they would have plenty of room for a growing family. In her mind Kate pictured something like the home she had grown up in. There were six bedrooms, three bathrooms, a playroom, and a large screened-in in porch all on a five-acre lot. In addition to the six bedrooms, there was a small room off the master suite that her dad had always used as an office. It would make a perfect nursery. They set the Labor Day family picnic at Ruth's and Charlie's as the time to tell their families about their decision to adopt.

Sunday morning of Labor Day weekend Kate, her sisters, and her mom were discussing details for the next day's get-together just before service started. The picnic was being held at Ruth's and Charlie's house because all the local parks were so crowded on Labor Day. Just as they moved to take their seats for the start of the service, they heard an ambulance go by with sirens blaring. As was his habit, Charlie took a moment to pray for the occupant of the ambulance even though he had no idea who it was. He knew his Heavenly Father knew whom he was praying for. About fifteen minutes later his cell phone vibrated. He slipped it out of his pocket to check the caller ID. When he saw it was from the local hospital, he quickly exited the sanctuary and answered the call. The unknown person he had just prayed for his brother Herb. He had suffered a massive heart attack. Since the congregation was still singing, he knew Pastor Alan would still be sitting in the front pew. Charlie slipped back into the sanctuary and walked quietly up to Pastor Alan and informed him of his brother's heart attack. He could feel his family's eyes on him. After talking to the pastor, he went to the pews where his family was sitting and let them know what had happened. Ruth gathered her things to leave as did several of his adult children. Charlie waved them back saying, "he is probably in ICU, and you won't be allowed in any way. Mom and I will go see how he is, and we will text you." They all looked at each other and knowing he was right, they stayed where they were lifting Uncle Herb and their parents in prayer. As Ruth and Charlie were leaving, they heard the song end and Pastor Alan telling the congregation about Herb. They knew that Pastor Alan would pray for all of them before he continued the service. When Ruth and Charlie arrived at the hospital, they went right to the emergency department. Going up to the desk they identified themselves as next of kin for Herbert Landers. The receptionist pointed to a room down the hall and asked them to wait there while she got someone to take them to Herb. She said he had already been moved to the ICU.

Ruth had just sat down while Charlie stared out the window praying when a doctor entered the room. He introduced himself and said, "I understand you are Mr. Landers' brother and his next of kin."

"Yes," Charlie answered. "His wife Helen died about five years ago in a car accident and they never had any children. How is he, doctor?"

The doctor took a breath and replied, "not good. He is unconscious. The heart attack happened at least an hour before he was found. I understand he owns a motel. The morning cleaning lady found him when she came into work. She said he has a very strict morning routine and based on how much of the routine was done, gave us the approximate time for the heart attack. He was barely breathing and unconscious when he was found. He never regained consciousness. Since arriving here his condition has deteriorated. He is being kept alive on life support, but there is no brain activity. There is no hope of recovery. Clinically he is brain dead."

Ruth stood and moved to where Charlie was standing, and he took her in his arms. The doctor kindly gave them a minute to process the news and then offered to take them to see Herb. As they followed the doctor down the hall, Charlie said to him, "if he is truly dead then you are not taking us to see him. If he is dead, he is in the presence of our Savior."

The doctor was a believer, but not sure of Charlie's beliefs, answered carefully. "Your brother was religious, should we notify a priest?"

"No." responded Charlie, "not religious and we don't need a priest. My brother was a born-again believer in the redemptive power of Christ's death on the cross. God promises in the Scripture

We are confident, I say, and would prefer to be away from the body and at home with the Lord. 2 Corinthians 5:8

"Amen," replied the doctor. "Then so you know it is my belief both medically and personally that your brother is already in the presence of the Lord. I'll take you to his body."

Charlie knew when he reached the ICU that as next of kin, he would be asked to agree to terminate life support. He knew he would do it because it was the right thing to do. His brother was with the Lord and didn't need machines to be breathing for his old body any longer. He turned to Ruth, "now, or let the kids come first?"

She thought for a minute. "He's already gone. They can do nothing here that they can't do at the funeral home. And there won't be any tubes or machines."

Charlie saw the wisdom in what she had said and turning to the doctor said, "can you give us about ten minutes, and then I will sign whatever forms are necessary."

"Of course," answered the doctor and left them alone while he went to get the necessary forms. Twelve minutes later he returned with a clipboard in his hand.

Charlie looked up and said, "we are as ready as we will

ever be." He signed the forms and handed them back to the doctor. The doctor told them they could stay or leave the choice was theirs. Charlie looked at Ruth. She didn't need to say anything, her face said it all. "We don't want to stay in the room. How long will it take?"

The doctor answered, "since I witnessed your signature hospital regulations require that I not be the one to turn off the machines. As soon as I can locate another doctor, maybe fifteen minutes?"

"Is there somewhere we can wait other than this room until it's over?"

"Absolutely," the doctor said. "Come right this way." He led them to a small lounge that was currently empty. As he left, he closed the door and switched the sign on the door from available to in use to prevent them from being disturbed.

He quickly paged another doctor who reviewed Herb's chart and checked the papers Charlie had signed. "It's the only decision that could be made," he said. Together the two doctors went into Herb's room. In a few minute,s all was quiet. Time of death 11:56 am. The original doctor said, "the family is waiting in the lounge, I will let them know."

The second doctor said, "I'll fill out the death certificate and arrange for him to be moved to the funeral home."

Ruth and Charlie stood when the door opened. "Is it over?" asked Charlie.

"It is," the doctor responded.

Ruth glanced at the clock. "If we leave now, we can text the kids to meet at our house after church. I'll call and have something delivered for lunch. Pizza or Chinese?"

"Let's go Chinese if you don't mind deciding what to order."

"No problem. When we all ordered Chinese a few months ago, I kept the paper that had everyone's choices. I spotted it in my purse just this week. I thought about throwing it out but for some reason, I didn't. I'll just use that to order now. I'll guess for Nate and Jenny." While Ruth called in the order for Chinese, Charlie sent everyone a text, please meet at our house right after church. We need to talk. Then he turned off his phone. When Ruth finished ordering, he suggested she turn off her phone too. That way if the kids try to call and ask what's going on, it will go right to voice mail and they will know our phones are off.

Soon everyone arrived in a line of cars. As always family included Joy, Dan, and Karen. Now it also included Eric. Nate had pulled into their driveway next door. When Nate and Jenny hesitated, Charlie called out, "you're family. This includes you. Come on over." When Ruth and Charlie broke the news, there were tears of course.

Then Zach said, "at least he's with Aunt Helen now." That seemed to start everyone reminiscing about the good times they had shared with Uncle Herb. By the time the Chinese food was delivered twenty minutes later they were all ready to eat.

They continued for a while talking about Uncle Herb and then Kate asked, "what about tomorrow?'

To which Charlie replied, "my brother would be offended if he thought we were going to cancel getting together because of this." They all laughed knowing he was right.

13

Things were taken care of quickly at the funeral home the next morning. To everyone's surprise, Herb had made all the arrangements for his funeral and burial shortly after Helen was killed. He was to be buried in a private ceremony tomorrow with a memorial service at the church on Friday. No visiting hours. That's how Herb wanted it. Charlie saw no reason to go against his brother's wishes. Charlie stopped by the motel Herb owned on his way home. Ruth had ridden ahead with Joe and Kate. At the motel he found that in the last twenty-four hours Herb's loyal staff had seen to everything that needed doing. Charlie thanked the staff and asked them to keep accurate records of their time and to keep things running smoothly for a couple of days until the will was read and he could see if provision had been made for the motel. He asked Rita to wait a minute as the rest of the staff left to carry on with their duties. Rita and her husband attended their church. Herb had often commented that Rita knew more about the workings of the motel than he did. Charlie asked Rita how they had covered the overnight hours the previous evening. She said she had covered them.

Charlie asked, "did you sit up all night?

"Well, yes," she admitted reluctantly.

"And you are here working this morning? Did anyone come in?"

"Not after ten last night."

"Is the room next door rented?"

"Not at present."

"Why don't you call your husband and the two of you stay in that room tonight? I'll drop off a baby monitor later. If you put one end here and the other in your room, you'll hear the bell. You can also leave a note on the office door where you can be found. I'd feel a lot better if you weren't here alone at night. The will is being read at eleven tomorrow morning following the burial. As soon as we are done at the lawyer's office, I'll stop by and let you know. "Did Herb pay everyone weekly or biweekly," Charlie asked?

"He paid us biweekly," answered Rita.

"And were you paid last week?"

"Yes, we were paid Friday."

"Great," said Charlie. "Hopefully, that gives me time to get the paperwork in place so everyone can be paid on time." This time when Charlie turned to go, he kept going until he reached the car. Turning back, he looked at the motel again and started developing an idea in his head. He drove slowly and took the long way home so excited about the possibilities he was envisioning that he wanted a little extra time. He would have to talk to Ruth first and see what Herb had outlined in his will but was excited to carry out the ministry with the hotel that Herb had started with Helen's life insurance money five years earlier. When he reached home, Ruth gave him a quizzical look. After thirty-two years of marriage, she could read him like a book. He kissed her and whispered, "later."

Zeke came into the room right then and asked, "how are things at the motel?"

"The staff is seeing that everything gets done," Charlie answered.

"Any idea what will become of the motel?" asked Zach who had followed his brother into the room.

"Nothing can be decided until the will is read tomorrow. Is everyone here, including Nate and Jenny? Can you ask everyone to join me in the living room?? Since we got done with the funeral home so quickly, let's have a family meeting so everyone knows what's happening this week."

Just as the last stragglers took a seat, the phone rang. Charlie left the room to take the call. He was only gone a few minutes. When he returned, he started by explaining, "the phone call was the lawyer confirming the appointment for the morning. The lawyer had a confusing request. He said Herb had recently changed his will and had asked that Nate and his family be there for the reading of the will. The lawyer said that Herb hadn't known their last name. He was planning to find it out at the Labor Day picnic and then call the lawyer to have it added to his will. The lawyer had no idea who the family was so had been unable to contact them. He wanted to know if we knew who the family is."

Joe said, "Uncle Herb was over for dinner one night when Nate, Jenny, and the kids were over. He thoroughly enjoyed them. It would be just like Uncle Herb to include them."

"Dan, Joy, Karen, and Eric you are invited to be there also." Charlie started the meeting by informing everyone about how things were being handled at the motel. He then checked to see if anyone had any questions about the funeral arrangements. When all the details of the funeral were clear to everyone, he closed the meeting in prayer.

14

The next morning, they all met at the lawyer's office about ten minutes before the scheduled time of 11:00 am. As the lawyer started to read the will, they were all shocked to learn that Herb had left behind a very sizable amount. The motel went to Charlie and Ruth. Herb had sold his home after Helen's death because there were too many memories of Helen in the home. He had used the proceeds from the sale to fix up the manager's apartment at the motel and moved in there. Then he had used Helen's life insurance money to remodel the motel rooms. He had turned the twelve rooms into six two-room efficiency suites. He had also added a community room and playground. These were rented to people who would otherwise be homeless. Many of the people were referred by social services. Those living there were given assistance to find jobs and/or permanent housing. Herb had also invited them to church and shared the gospel with each resident. As the lawyer started to read off the amounts of money that were being left to each of the five members of the motel staff, in a trust to each of the seven children already part of the family and for another potential ten children, Charlie interrupted.

"My brother had that much money," he asked? You said

he left $10,000 each to five staff and in trust for children. That adds up to $220,00, he had that much money?

The lawyer stopped reading and looked at Charlie. "Did you know he received a settlement after Helen was killed in the car accident?" questioned the lawyer.

"I remember Herb mentioning that because the other driver was intoxicated at the time of the accident the insurance company was going to sue," responded Charlie.

The lawyer continued, "not only was the other driver intoxicated, but he had no driver's license because he had been convicted three times of DWI. The settlement was $3.5 million. In addition, they both had two separate life insurance policies of $500,000 each. He invested all the money and has been living off the income from the sale of the house and the motel. His investments have done well. Two weeks ago, when he came in to add Nate, Jenny, and their kids to the will he arranged for all his investments to be readily available for cash."

Charlie was in shock. He could see similar looks of incredibility on the faces of everyone in the room. The lawyer continued to read Herb's will. "To Joy and Daniel Kanell, I leave $50,000 each. To Karen and Eric Walden; to Kate and Josiah Kannell; to Ezekiel and Leah Landers; to Zachariah and Lydia Landers: to Nathan and Jennifer Johnson I leave $50,000 each." The lawyer paused and looked at all their faces. They each had a look of complete shock. He had to hide a chuckle. He addressed all those who had just been named and said you do realize that this is each person, not each couple? They all just continued to stare at him. He didn't think any one of them could answer a simple question right at that moment. "The rest of my assets I leave to my brother Charlie and his wife Ruth." The lawyer finished up reading the last details of the will and sat back, smiling. "Herb said this would come as a shock to all of you and he left a letter addressed to Charlie and the family. I haven't seen the contents of the letter, but he said it would explain why he never told you about the amount of the settlement. You are welcome to stay here and read it since you are all together. If you need anything, please let me know."

Charlie stood and shook the lawyer's hand and said, "thank you for everything." As the lawyer and his secretary left the room some of the family came out of their daze and called out thanks.

They all sat down and waited expectantly as Charlie opened the letter. The letter was addressed to all of them. In the letter, Herb explained that he didn't want them to grieve, that he was happier than he had ever been in the presence of his Lord and reunited for all time with Helen. He would wait for the day when they were all united in heaven. He then explained that he had watched them all closely and no one had ever been in financial need, or he would have helped them out. He said he was proud of the way they all handled their finances and knew they would be good stewards of this money. He had waited because he felt this would be a good surprise amid the sorrow over his death. When Charlie finished the letter, he looked at each of the people in the room. No one knew what to say.

Finally, Dan joked, "he was trying to give us all heart attacks so we could join him in heaven." Everyone joined Dan in laughter and the shock of all that had just happened eased a little. The family all started to file out of the conference room.

Ruth whispered something to Charlie who then asked

for everyone's attention. "The next few days are going to be busy with the funeral and everything. Let's all get together at our house after church on Sunday. Nothing fancy. Everyone call in your family's order for pizza to be delivered to the house. Ruth and I will provide ice cream and toppings for ice cream sundaes. That includes everyone in this room and their kids. Afterward, we will put on a movie, play board games, take a nap, and just relax." Everyone agreed with the plan. When they reached the parking lot everyone called out goodbye and see you tomorrow and quickly headed home.

On their way home Charlie and Ruth stopped by the motel to let them know that salaries would be paid on time and to watch for a letter from the lawyer. He told them that Herb had left them each something and they would be receiving a certified letter soon with the details. He also posted a note by the time clock asking each of the staff to meet with him and Ruth next Tuesday at 11:00 am.

On the way home Charlie and Ruth stopped for coffee. They sat in silence for a few minutes sipping on their coffee each lost in thought over everything that had transpired in the last week. After about five minutes Ruth looked at her husband and said, "out with it." Charlie tried to give her his best look of innocence, but Ruth just laughed and said, "you don't fool me."

"OK, you're right. I want to sell the house to Kate and Joe. Their apartment is too small for the four of them. They'd never be able to adopt there. I want us to move to Herb's and continue the ministry he started."

WEDNESDAY, SEPTEMBER 7, 2011

With everything going on yesterday Joe and Kate hadn't called to confirm they were ready to start classes and move ahead with fostering to adoption. With Uncle Herb's generous gift there should be no problem with them purchasing a new, bigger home. Kate made the call to social services, while Joe sat at the table talking to Grace. Seeing the look on Kate's face Joe stopped talking to the baby and tuned into Kate's call. "Wait," said Kate, "Joe's right here. I'm going to put you on speaker. Now would you mind repeating what you just told me?"

"Hi Joe, this is Cheryl from the foster and adoption unit. I was just explaining to Kate that in the last week we have had four foster families retire and two more are moving out of state at the end of the month. That will leave us with very few places for new children coming into care. We have decided to offer a fast-track set of classes for those who have signed up for classes because they have already decided to foster or adopt. From talking to you I believe you have already decided to adopt and are willing to take an at-risk placement as long as there isn't visitation. Is that correct?"

"Yes," answered Joe and Kate together.

"Would you be interested and available to meet during the day for the next 2 to 3 weeks?

Joe pulled out his calendar. "We are free except for Thursday the 15th. The girls have an appointment with the specialist and that typically takes all day due to travel time."

"Great," said Cheryl. "There are eight other couples signed up for the initial orientation class tomorrow. There are three or four couples who I think have already decided fostering or adopting is for them. The others are interested but may need the full ten weeks to come to that decision. I am going to talk with them. If I can get two or three couples interested and available to fast-track, we will do it. I'd still like you to attend orientation tomorrow night. It will count towards your thirty required hours, and we can get those couples who are going to fast-track together to compare schedules. Will you be able to arrange childcare at such short notice?"

Kate answered, "it won't be a problem for Abby but since Grace is still nursing, we had planned to bring her with us."

"Great and absolutely bring Grace along."

As soon as she hung up the phone Kate called first her mom, then Jenny explaining the fast-track plan and that Cheryl hoped to have their home approved by the end of September. "Which means we had better get house hunting right away. Maybe we can find one that is available to rent for a month or two while we wait to close." Both her mom and Jenny were excited for them and assured Kate they would be available to help with Abby.

When Ruth hung up from Kate's call, she went and shared the news with Charlie. He responded with enthusiasm and said, "we need to decide on the house sooner rather than later."

"I agree with you, but we need to talk to the boys and make sure they don't have any objections. We don't want any hard feelings. And Jenny," she added. "We promised before God that she would be treated as a full daughter. Let's call the boys and see if we can meet at Zeke's."

While Ruth got ready to go Charlie called both their sons. When Ruth came out ready to go, he said "the boys and their families would meet them at Zach's in ten minutes."

"Zach's not Zeke's?" asked Ruth.

"Zach said Mark just went down for a nap. Zeke said Luke just woke up and nursed so they asked if we could meet at Zach's. I agreed."

When they arrived at Zach's, Ruth immediately reached out to hold her grandson Luke. Even though he was almost 3 weeks younger than Grace he was considerably bigger having weighed eight pounds three ounces at birth. As Ruth settled into the big rocker the rest found seats and looked expectantly at Charlie.

"Where's Kate and Joe?" asked Zeke.

"And Jenny and Nate?" added Zach.

"We decided it was best to meet with you guys first. If you approve, then we will meet with the others," explained Charlie. "And besides that, Nate is at work." He continued, "let's start with prayer." After praying Charlie began. "You all know about the ministry Herb has going at the motel. Your mom and I have talked. We would like to continue that ministry. Rita could probably keep it going, but we want to take it over with Rita's help of course. We want to move into Herb's place. We will probably add onto it since Herb only has one bedroom and a kitchenette."

"What about the house?" asked Zach. The idea of strangers in the house they grew up in or never having family dinners there just didn't feel right to any of them.

"We would like to sell it to Joe and Kate for $45,000 dividing that between your two families and Jenny and Nate. They are hoping to adopt and need a bigger place. You each own your homes as do Jenny and Nate. Kate called me this morning to tell me they are going to be able to fast-track their classes for adoption and will be certified by the end of the month, so they need to move somewhere bigger as soon as possible. This seems like the best solution."

"The house is too big just for dad and me," said Ruth. "Now that we are retired, we really want the opportunity to be involved in the ministry at Herb's motel. With Rita there we will still, be able to spend time with family and friends."

"I think it's a terrific plan," said Zach.

"I don't," said Zeke. Ruth and Charlie were taken aback by Zeke's statement. They had agreed that if any of the kids were against it, they would rethink the idea. Zeke didn't give them time to question his response but immediately followed up his statement with an explanation. "I don't want you to SELL it to Kate and Joe. With Uncle Herb's generosity, we certainly don't need the extra money. I say just give it to Kate and Joe, don't sell it to them."

"I agree," said Zach enthusiastically. I was just so relieved the house would stay in the family that I didn't even think about the money. "My only request is I get to see her face when you tell her. And make it soon please!"

"Ok, we will head to Jenny's now," said Ruth. Nate often comes home for lunch. If we can get their approval, we will invite everyone for lunch after church on Sunday and tell them then.

Sunday morning it was obvious to Kate that something was going on with their family. Kate tried asking her brothers, but they pretended they didn't know anything. Her parents insisted nothing was going on, But Kate wasn't convinced. She checked with Joe, and he agreed that something was apparently on the minds of Kate's family. He admitted asking Nate who insisted nothing was up.

Kate asked, "do you think your family knows anything?"

Joe answered, "my parents claim not to know, and I think I believe them. They don't look like they are hiding anything."

"If I could get Zach alone, I think he would tell me," Kate said. "He was never any good at keeping a secret. Lydia hasn't left his side for a second which only confirms to me that something is indeed up."

The music started then to signal the start of the service. Kate had a hard time concentrating on the message that morning. The rest of her family did too. Kate could tell by the look on her family's faces that whatever they were hiding was good news. She wasn't worried, just curious. She assumed it had to do with her and Joe since everyone else seemed to know. As the service ended, the family prepared to head for Ruth's and Charlie's. As the youth pastor, Joe had to stick around until everyone was gone. Kate would greet people for a while, then find a quiet place to nurse Grace. If Joe was busy, she took Abby and went into the now empty nursery. If he wasn't involved, he took Abby, and she went into his office. There was always the chance that someone would come back into the nursery looking for a forgotten item. Joe's office was more private, and Kate enjoyed the private time with Grace knowing that she was not likely to have another infant to nurse. She tried not to dwell on the thought and when it did creep up on her she would immediately pray and ask God for comfort. He always gave it, and she would deliberately think about what children they might be blessed with in the future. She also spent time praising God for the gift of Grace. She reminded herself that if they had found out that Abby's deafness was genetic before Grace was conceived, they might have come to the decision to adopt earlier, and she might not have Grace. Today Joe didn't have anything specific he needed to do, so he took Abby. Most of the church family had learned a few signs and would greet Abby as well as Joe. The interaction was great for her. Kate smiled at the picture they made as she headed for Joe's office. Her two-foot six-inch daughter with shoulder-length blond curls and big blue eyes that didn't miss anything was perched on her six-foot four-inch daddy's arm. Abby's light features were a contrast to Joe'sclose-cropped dark hair and brown eyes. She knew the curls were from Joe, even though Joe's couldn't be seen because he had just gotten a haircut. She liked his curls and loved to run her fingers through them. She never minded when things got busy and the time between haircuts stretched out long enough for the curls to come back. She smiled as she realized her daughter had finished eating and was asleep. And that she had managed to think about something other than what her family was hiding. When they reached her parents, they could see that everyone was there. They were usually last, but with a very good reason. God was using them to reach out for him.

As they entered Charlie's and Ruth's home, they could

see everyone gathered and waiting. It was obvious that Joe's family was in on the secret. As she looked around Kate smiled. "Ok, out with it, you guys. I know you are hiding something. It's not my birthday or Christmas." They enjoyed seeing Kate try to get the information, knowing how she would react when she finally found out.

When the laughter finally died down, Charlie said, "Ruth and I have an announcement to make."

Finally, thought Kate. Everyone quieted down and waited for Charlie to give the announcement, He turned to Joe and Kate and asked them, "have you found a house yet?"

"We've looked at a few but haven't found anything we like," answered Joe.

"What are you looking for," Charlie asked?

"Something with five bedrooms and a yard is the minimum requirement," Joe responded.

"We are looking for something like this house," said Kate referring to her parents' home. "That is the problem. We both know that this house would be perfect and compare everything else to it. And nothing comes close." Joe noticed the grins starting to spread around the room.

Charlie continued, "Ruth and I have decided to continue the ministry Herb started at the motel, to do it as a ministry we feel we need to live in Herb's apartment at the motel. It's a lot smaller than this place, which is too big for us, and the time we won't have to spend on upkeep we can spend enjoying our family and in ministry. Our original idea was to sell this place to Joe and Kate and divide the money among your siblings. However," and now he looked at Kate, "we wanted to talk to your brothers and sister first to make sure they didn't object. Well, they objected very strongly." Seeing the hope in his daughter's eyes fading quickly, he hurried on. "Kate, they didn't object to you and Joe having the house, only to us selling the house to you. They all agreed that since they all own their homes and are doing well financially, especially since Herb's generous gifts, they want us to transfer the title to you and Joe."

Kate looked around the room and saw everyone nodding and smiling. "It's too much," she said.

"Just use it for God and fill it with children," Ruth said.

With that Kate burst into tears and buried her head in Joe's chest. Joe held his wife as the tears ran down his cheeks too. He looked around at the family gathered here, many with tears in their eyes, and said, "thank you doesn't seem like enough to say, but we are so overwhelmed by how God has used all of you to bless us that I don't know what else to say."

Charlie, with great emotion, said, "let's pray." He thanked God for all those present and the closeness of this family.

16

Monday morning found Ruth and Charlie at the lawyers getting the paperwork started for changing the ownership of the house to Joe and Kate. They decided to stop at a local diner for lunch. In a spur-of-the-moment decision, they decided to call Pastor Alan and see if he and his wife could join them.

The pastor's wife, Elaine, answered the phone and said, "I've just taken something out of the refrigerator to heat up for lunch." After checking with her husband, she said, "I can put it right back in the fridge and we can meet you." They agreed to meet at a local diner in ten minutes.

When Pastor Alan and Elaine arrived at the diner, Ruth and Charlie were already seated and waiting. "Sorry to keep you waiting," apologized Pastor.

"You haven't kept us waiting, we just got here ourselves."

They kept the conversation light and general until after they had all placed their orders. Then Pastor Alan looked at Ruth and Charlie and asked them how they were doing.

"Alright," Charlie said. "Have you talked to Joe this morning?"

"No," said the pastor. "We both agreed that Monday mornings would be our mornings to work at home. After the busyness of the weekend, Sunday in particular, we decided to take it easy Monday mornings and meet at 2:00 pm to pray and look ahead to the new week."

"Good plan'" said Ruth.

"Why," asked Pastor? Charlie looked at Ruth and grinned. "Does this have anything to do with why your whole family wasn't paying a bit of attention to the sermon yesterday?" joked Pastor Alan.

Charlie chuckled and said, "it does. Had you heard that Herb left the motel to Ruth and me? And also, a sizeable inheritance to each of our kids and our grandkids?"

"No," said the pastor, "I figured the motel would go to you two, but I didn't realize he had the resources to leave gifts to everyone let alone sizeable ones."

Charlie continued, "we have decided to move to the motel and continue the ministry Herb started. We are going to change the name to Haven of Hope. We meet with the Department of Social Services this afternoon."

Elaine had sat quietly taking in all they were proposing. Now she spoke up and said, "what about that big, beautiful home of yours?"

Ruth answered with tears in her eyes, "our original plan was to sell it to Joe and Kate keeping the price low enough to not strain their budget. However, our other kids were adamant we do not sell it to Joe and Kate."

She could see the shock on Alan's and Elaine's faces. "They didn't want Joe and Kate to have it?" Elaine asked.

"Oh, they didn't object to Joe and Kate having the house," Ruth continued. "They objected to our selling them the house. We had planned to divide the price of the house so they would all benefit from it. Our kids insisted we give the house to Joe and Kate. They say God has provided for them and Joe and Kate need a bigger house. We sign the papers on Thursday to transfer ownership of the house to Joe and Kate."

The waitress brought their meals at that moment and Elaine and Alan were glad she did. All they had just heard had left them speechless. Alan offered the blessing over the food, and they spent the rest of the meal in light conversation.

The appointment at Social Services went very well. The worker was enthusiastic that Herb's ministry was going to be continued.

That evening Charlie couldn't find Ruth and went looking for her. He found her upstairs in the bedroom that used to be Kate's. He watched her for a minute as she stood with her eyes closed and head bowed. She didn't see him as she moved down the hall to Zach's old room. When she left Zach's room to head to Zeke's she spotted him. He took her in his arms and asked if she was having second thoughts.

"No," she said pulling back, not at all.

"Then what are you doing?"

"I'm praising God for the person the child who used to have this room has become. I'm also praying for the future occupant that whoever uses this room will learn of our Father's love and want to serve him all their days."

Charlie struggled to speak around the lump in his throat, "let's pray together."

Tuesday morning Kate looked up from packing a box when she heard the back door open. "Hi," she greeted Joe, "I didn't expect you home until this afternoon." Fast-track classes were going to meet from 1:00 to 4:30 four days a week.

"The board of deacons at church met last night without telling me. It seems someone told them about our upcoming move and our desire to adopt more children. They have decided that for the next two weeks I am only to do the minimum. I'm still doing youth group and my part of Sunday services, but no visitation, no working in the office to take routine phone calls. They said I should study for youth group lessons at home. They want to support and help us in any way they can to help us get moved and settled. They have already lined up people to help your parents move for both Friday and Saturday. They have lined up people to shampoo carpets, paint, and whatever we want to be done for next week. The following weekend they have people scheduled to help us move. I also have a list of women who are ready and willing to help pack or watch kids either here or at their homes starting tomorrow. And supper will be delivered every day for the next two weeks."

Kate muttered,

Philippians 4:19
And my God shall meet all your needs
according to his riches of his glory in Christ
Jesus.

Kate looked up at Joe with tears in her eyes, "I was
just asking God how we would get everything done. I was
asking if maybe we should postpone adoption classes to the
spring classes. I just wasn't sure I could handle anything
else right now. And he had already provided, isn't God
good?"

Joe pulled Kate into his arms and kissed the top of her
head. "He is indeed good. Now, how about you take the
list and call Roberta. She is coordinating everything. She
wants to know what we want to eat and what is the best
way to help. She assumed you would want at least Grace
watched here or close enough to be brought over when she
is ready to nurse."

Fifteen minutes later, Kate hung up the phone and just
sat for a full minute without moving going over in her
mind all that had just been arranged. Two women would
show up at her house every morning at 9:00 and would
help in any way they could. They would stay until noon
packing, watching the girls, even doing dishes or laundry,
if that was what would be the biggest help. From 1:00 to
4:30 a different pair of ladies would arrive to help. They
would watch Abby and continue packing while Joe and
Kate were at adoption class. Dinner would be delivered at
5:15 each afternoon. Whenever they were ready the help
would switch to the new house. God had it all worked out!

After lunch, they attended foster care and adoption class. Cheryl started by explaining that "foster children could be placed with little or no warning. We will call you when we have a child or sibling group we think might fit in your family. Most of the time when we call, the child has already been picked up by a worker from our agency. If you don't agree that the child will fit in your family, you are always free to say no. It is much better for you to say no before the child is placed than to take a child you don't think is a good fit for your family and then two weeks down the road, the child has to be moved to another home. If you say yes, the worker may bring the child straight to you. We have had kids arrive at their foster home fifteen minutes after the call is made. Usually, you will have an hour. Keep in mind that children often come with the clothes on their backs. We have foster parents who have gone to the thrift store and keep two outfits and a pair of pajamas in each size on hand. The kids sometimes, not always, arrive very dirty. You will want to give them a bath, and you will want clean clothes before you take them out shopping for new clothes. If you are willing to take babies or toddlers, it might be a good idea to keep a bottle and a sippy cup on hand. Joe and Kate were impressed with how practical the classes seemed to be. They were anxious for more adoption information. If you are only interested in adopting, you will have more time. From the time you are matched with a child until that child comes home is usually several months of visiting back and forth before the child comes home to stay. There is another option for those interested in adoption. If you are willing to take an at-risk adoption placement. In those cases, a child is placed with you as a foster child with the intention that the child will be freed for adoption and can then just stay with you. It prevents the trauma of two moves for the child and you get a good chance to know the child before you commit to adopting." One of the other couples asked her to explain how exactly a child gets classified as an at-risk adoption placement. "In July we had two little boys come into foster care. The parents are both dead. There is no extended family who can care for these children. When we placed them with a family, who hopes to adopt them, they were not legally free to be adopted. There was no guarantee that they would ever be free, but the circumstances pointed to the fact that it was highly likely they would be freed for adoption. Understanding that there wasn't a certainty a family took the chance and took the kids."

"Did they get freed?" asked a member of the class.

Cheryl grinned, "as a matter of fact as I was leaving the office today, the phone rang. I'll be honest I almost didn't go back and answer it. But I was certainly glad I did. It was the judge's office calling saying a case had been settled out of court and he had an opening and would sign the papers to allow the kids to be adopted tomorrow morning at 11:00 if I could bring the children to court. I agreed without even calling the foster parents. I tried calling but they weren't home. I'll call them this evening." She noticed the grin on Joe's and Kate's faces and confirmed she was speaking about Jenny and Nate when she said with mock fierceness, "and don't you two dare tell them. I want the privilege." Seeing the confused look on some of the faces in the room Cheryl explained that Joe and Kate were good friends with the foster parents.

"Jenny's at our house watching Abby and cooking supper. Nate gets home at 4:30 and we'll have supper together."

Joe added, "you will want to be sure you call immediately after we are done. Kate does not have a poker face. Jenny will take one look at her and knowing where we have been, will figure something is up." Seeing Kate's face, the rest of the class laughed along with Joe and Kate. They could tell Joe knew what he was talking about.

Cheryl agreed with Joe's statement too. She laughed and asked, "how long it would take you to get home?"

Joe said, "about 10 minutes."

"Alright," said Cheryl. "Don't stop on the way. I'll give you 12 minutes and then I'll call. You can have a minute's fun before I call." The whole class applauded the plan before getting back down to business. After class Kate and Joe along with Grace who still nursed too frequently to be left with a sitter, hurried out of class to calls of have fun. They laughed as they both hurried up the sidewalk. Nate was already there and gave them a funny look. Jenny walked into the room and took one look at Kate's face before demanding, "out with it, what is going on." Kate and Joe looked at each other and burst out laughing just as Jenny's phone rang. Jenny turned to answer it calling over her shoulder to Kate, "I know you're up to something."

Joe turned to Nate and said, "you might want to follow her and ask her to put the call on speaker." Nate looked puzzled but followed his advice. Kate and Joe not wanting to miss the excitement followed. They caught up in time to see Jenny put the phone on speaker and hear Cheryl ask if they were free tomorrow at 11:00 to meet with her.

Jenny looked at Nate who nodded yes. "We can if I can get a sitter for the kids."

"Oh, just bring them all. You can bring those two with the silly grins and their two kids also if you want."

Jenny looked at Joe and Kate and saw they were about to burst. "What is going on?" she demanded.

"Not much, just that the judge is going to sign the papers so you two can adopt Jackson and Andrew if you can have them here at 11:00," Cheryl said.

Jenny screamed and then dropping the phone, was in Nate's arms with tears running down her face saying over and over, "thank you, Jesus, praise God, thank you, Jesus."

Kate picked up the phone and thanked Cheryl saying we will all be there in the morning. She said goodbye and hung up the phone. Jenny was starting to get herself pulled together turned and asked how they knew. Joe explained about Cheryl using Jenny's and Nate's situation to explain an at-risk placement without using their names and that they had guessed who she was talking about. "She said she tried to call but it was probably when you were driving over here. She was going to call you this evening," Joe said, "but I told her one look at Kate's face and you'd know something was up." They all laughed.

Turning to Jenny, Kate asked, "do you need to do anything tonight to be ready for tomorrow?"

"No, I did laundry yesterday. We can all wear what we wore on Sunday. I'll have time to give everyone a bath in the morning. The kids were having so much fun playing tonight that I didn't have the heart to break up their fun for a bath."

Joe asked Nate, "do you work in the morning?"

Nate responded, "I'm not scheduled to go in until 3 pm. The other manager asked me to switch for tomorrow so he could go to his son's soccer game. I am off in the morning. Isn't it amazing how God works things out?"

18

Wednesday morning Kate was working on getting breakfast ready. Grace was sitting in her infant seat on the table. Joe came into the kitchen with Abby placing her in her highchair. As Joe turned around to say good morning to Grace, he bumped a stack of pans sitting on the counter waiting to be packed. When they hit the floor with a loud clatter both girls jumped, and Grace began to cry. Kate and Joe looked at each other, hardly daring to breathe. Kate whispered, "she heard that."

Joe said, "I think so, too."

"I've thought she heard other things, too," said Kate. "I've noticed her reacting to loud noises but was afraid to say anything and get our hopes up. I'm so excited to take her to see the specialist tomorrow."

The next morning, they left for the doctor's appointment at about 8:30. Both girls had appointments. They were eager to have Grace's hearing fully evaluated. They were also anxious to discuss Abby's progress with both the doctor and Carla. Abby was making great gains in her ability to understand spoken language. When she was with someone who didn't sign, she could follow their speech. Kate and Joe continued to sign and speak at the same time.

115

However, she had yet to make a sound or try to speak in the three months since receiving the hearing aids. If Grace could hear as they were hoping, they were wondering if they should stop signing to Abby in hopes it would encourage her to speak.

When they arrived, Abby didn't want to get out of the car.

She just kept signing, "no, no, no."

"Let's go see Carla," Kate encouraged. Abby enjoyed working with Carla.

Finally, Abby pointed to her hearing aids and signed, "mine." When Kate assured her the hearing aids were hers to keep, Abby was ready to go.

When they got inside, the first thing to happen was Grace's hearing evaluation. When it was done, the technician assured them that Grace's hearing was perfect. Next, they met with Carla who reassured them that there was nothing to worry about concerning Abby's lack of vocalization. "Children this age often have better receptive language than expressive language." Seeing their puzzled look, she explained "they can understand more of what they hear than they can say. Don't worry," she assured them. "I have a feeling that when Abby starts speaking, she will be a chatterbox!"

"How well do you think she hears?" Joe asked.

"Not perfectly," said Carla, "but well enough to function as a hearing-impaired child, not as a deaf child. It's important that whoever speaks to her does it from the front." To illustrate she wrote something on a piece of paper and asked Joe to stand behind Abby and read the paper in a normal voice.

Abby was busy playing with a toy. Joe stood behind her

and read from the paper, "do you want a cookie?" Hearing him behind her, Abby turned around and looked at him questioningly.

"Try again," Carla instructed.

Joe looked at Abby and asked, "Do you want a cookie?" Abby immediately dropped the toy and signed, "yes, please." Carla handed her the cookie.

As Abby ate the cookie, Carla explained that because they had always spoken when signing Abby had already learned some lip-reading. Abby heard her dad's voice behind her and turned to check it out. She didn't understand his words until she was looking at him. When she was facing him, she could understand them in part because she knew she was being spoken to and paid closer attention and in part because she was watching his lips.

The next week was very busy for Kate and Joe, even with all the help from their extended families and their church family. Abby didn't have the language skills to understand what was happening. She was becoming very clingy. Joe and Kate hoped once the move was complete, she would relax. They tried to show her exactly what was happening but that only seemed to upset her more. Jenny tried to take Abby to her house to play with Sammy, but Abby just kept asking for mommy and daddy. She signed mommy and daddy so many times, that Jenny was afraid her arm would be sore for days. In the end, Jenny took Abby back to Kate's and Joe's apartment after only an hour. Saturday, they spent the day at the house moving Ruth's and Charlie's things to Herb's apartment at the motel. Ruth and Charlie had offered to leave much of the furniture as Herb's apartment was nicely furnished. Joe and Kate had considered it but seeing Abby's confusion they thought it was better to completely remove all of Ruth's and Charlie's furniture. They were afraid that if she saw grandma's and grandpa's things, she would look for them too. Ruth and Charlie decided to use the extra furniture to update the suites. Anything they didn't need they would give away. They were all glad for Sunday and a day of rest. The weather was glorious that day, so they decided to pick up buckets of chicken and go to the lake for a picnic.

Monday morning arrived and so did the work crew of church members. The kitchen had been freshly painted about 6 months ago and Kate liked the color. The three women assigned to the kitchen made quick work of scrubbing down the entire kitchen. While they were busy in the kitchen, other crews were in the bedrooms painting. Kate had decided to turn the office off the master bedroom into a nursery for Grace for the present time. She had picked a soft light pastel green for the walls and planned to decorate them with butterflies in a variety of pastel colors. They had decided to paint Abby's room purple, and another bedroom was being painted pink and would eventually be Grace's room. They had debated what to do with the other three bedrooms. Hoping to adopt at least two boys they thought of painting and decorating all three of the extra bedrooms for boys. In the end, they decided to paint one room blue, one room green, and the third they would paint cream. The master bedroom would also be painted cream. When Joe went to pick up the paint the previous Friday, Kate had opted to stay home. She gave Joe instructions to be sure a pick a pretty pastel green for Grace's nursery and a more boyish green for the empty bedroom. Joe looked at Kate quizzically and asked her if she was sure she shouldn't go, and he'd stay with the kids? She had laughed and said she trusted him and besides what would he do when Grace got hungry? In the end, reason won out and Joe went with Nate while the women and children stayed home and made plans to decorate. Kate was thrilled with Joe's choices.

On Monday morning as she saw the colors being applied to the walls by their volunteer painters, she could envision the rooms decorated and ready for children. As she walked from one room to the next, she prayed for the children who would occupy each room. She prayed for Abby, Grace, and the children she trusted God to send their way. As she prayed for Abby, she wondered how she was doing. Joe's parents had taken Abby for the day. Abby had often spent the day at nana's and papa's house. They hoped that she would be able to enjoy her time with them and have a good day. The poor little girl had had a rough week not understanding why her parents were putting things in boxes. Joe and Kate had thought about leaving the rooms other than the bedrooms the same color. However, they felt it would be more their home and less Ruth's and Charlie's if they painted everything except the kitchen. Kate and her mom had picked out the color for the kitchen and Kate decided to stick with it. By noon on Monday, the painting crew had finished the first coat in all the rooms. They were just finishing cleaning their brushes when lunch arrived. It had been arranged to have trays of meat and cheese and some rolls delivered for lunch. In addition, they brought chips, cookies, and drinks. Lunch was a joyous occasion. The members of the church loved their young youth pastor and his family and were thrilled to be able to help. Kate and Joe were humbled by the number of people who had come to help and the amount of work that had been accomplished that morning. After lunch was over the crew went back to work shampooing carpets, scrubbing floors, and cleaning windows and by supper, the house was ready to move in. Just before everyone left Joe gathered them in the empty living room now painted a light tan to match their brown furniture and asked them to join him in prayer. As they were locking the door to head home, Joy called to let them know Abby was having a great day. The complete change of scenery had been good for her and asked if she could spend the night. Since she had done so in the past, Joe and Kate readily agreed. They drove across town to their apartment still marveling at all that had been accomplished that day.

As they were eating the supper that had been delivered, Kate asked Joe "what do you think about going shopping for curtains and other things for the new house.

Joe responded, "since Abby is at my parents' for the night it's a great idea." They quickly finished eating. Joe cleaned up while Kate fed Grace and headed out.

They stopped at a furniture store first planning to buy a new bed for Abby. Because her bedroom at the apartment was so small, they had kept her in a toddler bed. They wanted to get her a twin bed for her new room. Kate was looking at the twin beds with white headboards. She turned to say something to Joe and found he had wandered over to look at some sturdy brown bunk beds. "Are you thinking of them for Abby?" she questioned,

"No," Joe answered. "I was thinking about getting two sets of the darker brown and putting one set each in the blue room and the green room. See they come apart and can be used as single beds too. Then I thought we could get the lighter set and put it in the cream room. Those rooms are all big enough for two children. If we ever needed to put two children in a room, we would be able to have a matching set."

"Great idea!" Kate agreed. They saw a salesman approaching.

Joe smiled and whispered to Kate, "this is going to be one surprised salesman." They were surprised to learn the store delivered. In the end, they bought a bed for Abby, the three sets of bunks, a dresser to match each bed, and a dining room table and chairs. The new house had both a large eat-in kitchen and a big dining room. Their current table would go in the kitchen and now they would have something for the dining room. They arranged to have everything delivered the next morning and headed out to the department store. At the department store, they picked out new bedding and curtains for Abby in a print of cute baby animals. They found a jungle pattern for the green room and a pattern with cars and trucks for the blue room. They weren't sure what they wanted to do with the cream-colored room and had decided to leave it for another day since Grace was starting to fuss. Joe said, "I'll grab pillows and check out. You go-ahead to the car and feed Grace, and I'll meet you there."

Kate agreed and went out with the baby who was getting louder with each step. She finished feeding Grace about the same time Joe finished loading the packages into the trunk. She looked at him and wondered for a minute what he was up to, but forgot to ask when Joe said, "do you want to stop for a milkshake?"

Kate responded with one word, "strawberry." Joe laughed and Kate soon joined in. Joe pulled into the drive-through lane at the fast-food restaurant and ordered a strawberry for Kate and chocolate for himself. As they sipped their shakes, Kate mentioned that sometime in the next couple of weeks they needed to make a trip to the mall. Abby needed some new things and she wanted to check out the clearance racks for children that might come their way. Joe agreed that it should work into their schedule after the move.

When they got back to the apartment, Kate took the sleeping Grace in to lay her down in her bed. When she came back into the kitchen, Joe was bringing in the store bags. "Oh," said Kate surprised, "I thought you would probably just leave them in the car to take to the house in the morning." She looked at Joe. He had that look again like he was up to something. "Ok, Joe, what's going on?" she demanded.

"Nothing," he said too quickly, "I thought you would want to sort what we bought and pack it according to which room it goes in before we take it over."

"I guess," she said not convinced he wasn't up to something. She began pulling things out of the bags. As she pulled out one bedding set, she squealed and looked at Joe. He had a big grin on his face. "You were hiding something." She looked closely at the bedding set in her hands. It was Noah's ark print and could easily be for a girl or a boy depending on the accessories they put with it. Peeking in the bags she saw that Joe had bought two complete sets. "I didn't see these," she said.

Joe responded, "there was a clearance section over by the pillows and there were just two of these left. I thought you might like them." She threw her arms around her husband.

"They're perfect," she said. "Thank you for the surprise. You talk about my poker face. I knew something was up."

19

Tuesday morning the work crew showed up at Joe's and Kate's apartment at about 8:30. Joe was surprised to see them. "I thought we were meeting at the house at 9:00?"

Kate's brother Zeke was part of the crew today and it looked like he had been chosen as spokesman. Zeke said to Joe and Kate, "we finished everything at the house, and we are wondering if there is any reason not to start moving things in today? Why wait until Friday and Saturday?"

"Well, Kate and the women have most of the things packed so I guess we are ready enough. What about a truck?"

"We have three guys with trucks on standby at the church waiting to see if you agree with the plan."

Joe laughed. "Do you even need Kate and me? It looks like you have everything covered."

Zeke laughed and said, "just trying to help."

"Thanks, everyone," Joe said. "Let's move!"

Zeke called the guys on standby and said, "the move is on." The crew had it all worked out. Each truck and the guys working with it took a room. They decided to start with the kitchen, master bedroom, and living room. Within the hour the first truck was on the way to the new house. While the men were loading up the trucks, a crew of women was packing up the last of the things in each room. By eleven the apartment was empty. Kate and Joe decided it was time to head over to the new house. Nate and Jenny were at the new house directing things there. Kate took a last look around the now-empty apartment, knowing she would be back to clean in a day or two. Then picking up Grace she headed out the door, knowing that for now, the priority was to get enough unpacking done to function in the new house.

At the new house, she walked in the back door and entered the kitchen. She stood still and stared. The kitchen was completely unpacked. Even her pictures were hung on the wall and a dish towel was on the rack by the sink. She entered the dining room, and the curtains were hung. The room, of course, was empty. The furniture was being delivered later this morning. She continued to walk through the house. In every room, it was the same. Not a box was in sight. The kids' rooms had pictures on the walls that she had never seen before. Someone must have given them to decorate the rooms for the new kids they hoped God would send their way. The new curtains were hanging at the windows, but the rooms stood empty waiting for the arrival of the new furniture. She looked around for the new bedding and found it on the closet shelves. Joe was talking to some of the work crew assuring them that thanks to Uncle Herb, they did have furniture for the empty rooms. "In fact," he said, "it should be here by lunch." As if on cue the truck from the furniture store pulled up. It was followed by the pizza delivery van. Joe noticed that there were plates, napkins, cups, and drinks set out on the picnic table. Nate took charge of getting the pizza ready to serve and then led everyone in prayer. Joe led the way into the house showing the delivery man what rooms things went into. After lunch, most of the crew left. A few men stayed to put the new beds together. As soon as the beds were put together one of the women who had remained made up the bed with the new bedding. By 4:00 Kate and Joe were alone with Grace in their new home. They knew that Abby would be home in about a half-hour. They walked from room to room thanking God for his goodness. When they got to the bedrooms, they hoped would hold their new children, they prayed that God would send the right children at the right time to fill these rooms.

Soon they heard Joy and Dan pull into the driveway. They went out to greet them and Abby. As soon as they saw Abby, they could see that the time away had been good for her. She was signing so fast they could hardly keep up with her and decipher her sentences. They did catch "Abby new house" and "Abby new bed" a couple of times.

Kate gave her a big hug and then set her down so she could sign. "Yes, Abby this is your new home." She took her into the house and Abby looked at the familiar stuff in the kitchen and seemed to take comfort in the familiar things. They went through the dining room. Abby signed, "pretty." When they got to Abby's room, her eyes took in her toys and books and clothes. Then she saw the new bed and bedding. She looked at Kate and Joe and signed, "my pretty."

"Yes. Abby." her mom told her. "This is your pretty, new room."

Abby went running out of the room and back towards the kitchen. She spotted her suitcase by the back door where Dan had left it. She quickly opened it and took out her special blanket and the stuffed dog from her birthday and running back to her room she put them on her bed.

The adults laughed and Kate said, "any doubts that she understands this is her room?"

The next afternoon at class, Cheryl gave each couple a questionnaire to fill out during the first half-hour. It covered expectations, fears, hopes, and plans for each couple in terms of fostering and adopting. Cheryl collected the questionnaire and told them they would be used in the following class. She then invited any couple who felt comfortable doing so, to share why they were interested in fostering or adopting and what age and gender they were hoping for. One couple shared that now that their children were teens, they missed having little ones around. They didn't care if the children were boys or girls but desired only preteens. They were only interested in fostering because once their youngest graduated in 5 years, they wanted to travel. They also shared that because one of their children was recently married and another one planning a wedding, they saw grandkids in the future and wanted to be able to enjoy them. Another couple shared that they only wanted to adopt and would only consider children that were totally free. Joe and Kate explained they were interested in adopting children under 6 years of age. They preferred boys because they had two girls but weren't against a sibling group that included a boy and a girl. They said they had decided they would accept at-risk placements if there was no visitation with the biological family. After everyone had had a chance to share, Cheryl went on to tell them, "The agency took their feelings and desires into consideration when they placed children. That doesn't mean we will never call you with children outside of your desired preferences. But keep in mind you can always say no. Sometimes we have a child or a sibling group come into care, and we have no open beds in homes that have expressed their desire for that age child. For example, we might have a 13-year-old boy who needs a foster home. None of the homes with room wanted 13-year-olds, so we might call on you," she said indicating the couple who wanted preteens, "and ask you to consider. Or we might have a 2-year-old girl come in who is an at-risk placement. If we don't have a home with room to match, we might call Joe and Kate. All we ask is that you consider these placements and answer in a way you are comfortable with. Don't answer yes because you are so anxious for a child you will take one who doesn't fit in with your family. Keep in mind that the child you really want may come along the next month. We don't want you to traumatize the first child by asking we remove that child for the new one. Let's take a break," announced Cheryl. Over coffee and cookies, the families chatted about what they had heard and discussed that afternoon. After the break, they went over some of the regulations of foster care and adoption.

20

The rest of the week flew by. Ruth and Charlie had called. They were settled in their new home. Abby had adjusted very well for which Kate and Joe were very thankful. Grace was now 3 months old and alert. She was staying awake longer now and Abby was really taking an interest in her baby sister. Grace watched her big sister or parents whenever they were in the room. She still nursed every 3 hours during the day. If Kate fed her just before going to bed, she often slept until 5:30 or 6:00 the next morning. Kate was catching up on her rest. Sunday afternoon Kate and Joe decided to take advantage of a beautiful September day and take the girls for a walk. Kate was getting Grace ready when Joe came in and asked, "do you want the double stroller, two single strollers, one stroller, and the front pack or what?"

Kate thought for a minute and responded, "let's take the double stroller. That way Abby can walk if she wants and one of us will be free to hold her hand and if she gets tired on the way back, she can go in the stroller."

"Good thinking," Joe agreed and went to get the stroller out of the car and ready to go.

Monday afternoon at class Cheryl set up times for home

visits for the following week. She would be out to Joe's and Kate's on Monday morning.

Tuesday morning Joe met with Pastor Alan at the church. When he came home for lunch, Kate reminded Joe that had never made a trip to the mall. After the news that Grace could hear, they had completely forgotten about their plans to stop at the mall. The girls, especially Abby needed some new clothes and there were probably sales at this time of year. Joe agreed so they had a quick lunch and headed out the door. By 1:00 they were at the mall. They had decided to bring two single strollers to the mall. The double stroller was bulky and hard to maneuver in stores. As they had expected, several stores were having clearance sales and Kate was able to find what she needed for the girls. At one point Grace started to fuss a little so Joe started walking around with her while Kate finished picking out new clothes for the girls. When she finished, she looked around for Joe. One good thing about a tall husband was he was easy to spot! She made her way over to him pushing Abby in the stroller with outfits hanging from the stroller and socks and pajamas piled on top. Joe looked up as she approached and grinned sheepishly. "The clearance prices are so good it won't cost much more to get some clothes for the boys here than at the thrift store."

Kate's face immediately lit up and she looked at Joe and said, "I love you." They began to look together and ended up getting two pairs of pants, two pairs of shorts, two T-shirts, socks, two pairs of pajamas, a sweatshirt, and a package of underwear in every size from 12 months to 6 for under $200. The clerk looked at them with a funny look as they paid for their purchases. They could tell she was dying to ask why they were buying all the boy's clothes when they had two little girls. If there hadn't been a line behind them, they would have told her. As they were leaving Joe took pity on her and said, "we are going to be foster parents."

As they were leaving Kate looked at Joe and asked, 'foster parents?'

"It was the easiest way to explain and technically if we take an at-risk placement, we are foster parents until the child is freed for adoption. I couldn't stand to leave with her wondering," Joe said, and they both laughed.

Joe buckled Abby into her car seat and handed her a snack. He then loaded all their bags and the strollers into the back of the car while Kate buckled Grace's car seat into the base.

When they arrived home Kate took the girls into the house while Joe started unloading all their purchases. He came in the door with the first load and called out to Kate, "Where do you want them?"

"Why don't you put them in the Noah's ark room for now?

"The girls' things too," he asked?

"Yes," Kate answered, "that way I can sort everything out when the girls are in bed."

The next afternoon was their last foster care/adoption class. The class had agreed to meet for six hours and finish everything up.

21

SEPTEMBER 28, 2011

Wednesday was long but it went well. They had arranged to bring both girls with them along with a teenage sitter. Cheryl had arranged for the girls to be in a room next to their meeting room. When Grace needed to eat, Kate would be right there. Abby and Grace did well with the sitter. Cheryl invited the girls and the babysitter to join the adults at lunch. Abby went around the room teaching everyone signs and generally being delightful. Grace was a regular in class and she was big enough now that she was able to be held by others. She shared smiles all around.

Cheryl announced, "my supervisor is going on maternity leave a week from Monday and will be out a minimum of 8 weeks. She has cleared my schedule of everything except getting your home studies done. If my supervisor doesn't go into early labor, all your home studies will be done by the end of next week. We will schedule a time for each of you to come into the office and sign your completed home study." The class cheered this news. When everyone had quieted down again, she thanked everyone for the willingness to fast track their classes. She said, "as soon as I finish the home studies, you will be hearing from me."

Joe picked up Grace in her car seat while Kate took Abby's hand and the diaper bag. The babysitter grabbed the bin of toys and they all headed out to the car. After dropping off the sitter, Joe headed to Hope Haven. Ruth and Charlie had invited them to dinner. Abby was delighted to see he grandparents and was signing something so quickly no one was catching all of it. Kate encouraged her to slow down. Because Abby tended to invent signs she didn't know, she was sometimes difficult to understand. Kate finally figured out she was telling grandma and grandpa about her pretty new bedroom. It took a couple of repetitions, but they finally figured out she was also telling about the rooms for her brothers. Abby's sign for brother they discovered was a combination of boy me. Joe and Charlie took the two girls into the living room, while Kate and Ruth went to the kitchen to put the finishing touches on dinner. Abby picked out a toy from the box Ruth and Charlie kept for the grandkids. Joe took Grace out of her car seat and Charlie immediately reached for her. He settled into his favorite chair with Grace cuddled in his arms. Joe silently praised God that their families accepted the girls completely and totally despite Abby's hearing loss. He knew that not all parents of special needs children were so blessed. Many times, a child with a disability caused division in a family when someone in the extended family refused to treat that child as a valuable member of the extended family. He was glad that none of the adults treated Abby any different because of her deafness. Joe and Charlie talked about adoption class. Joe's eyes took on a sparkle as he told Charlie about the previous day's shopping trip.

"Wait a minute," Charlie said, "I thought your home study wasn't finished yet?"

"It isn't," Joe responded.

"Then how did you know what size to buy?" Charlie wanted to know.

Joe grinned sheepishly and responded, "we didn't know what size. We bought a few things in every size, trusting God to send us children."

"And if he doesn't?" Charlie asked.

"Then," Joe responded, "there are kids in this family, our church and town who will benefit." Charlie smiled and nodded his head in agreement. He was very proud of his son-in-law and his daughter and their ability to trust God.

At that moment Ruth came into the room and said, "time to eat." Charlie and Joe stood to go eat.

Joe went to Abby and signed and said, "time to eat." Abby stood and put the toy she was playing with back in the box and headed for the kitchen. Joe lifted her into the booster Ruth kept for grandkids, Kate took Grace from her dad and laid her in the playpen that stood in the corner of the kitchen. After Charlie prayed the food was passed around. When Kate finished cutting Abby's chicken and had her settled, she turned to her dad and asked how he liked the motel business.

Charlie responded, "I don't think I would like to run a traditional motel but the way we have set it up for ministry is very fulfilling. We have a young couple in unit three that you will meet at church Sunday. His company transferred him here and their new house won't be ready for at least six weeks. They weren't looking forward to unpacking for six weeks if they could find a short-term rental and then repacking. They considered staying in a hotel for six weeks, but it would have used up most of their savings. Someone recommended us. Since our units are totally furnished, they put their things in storage. There's a single lady in unit one who keeps to herself. She pays by the week, stopping in every Monday. Said she doesn't know how long she'll stay."

Ruth added, "she doesn't have a car and depends on the bus. I offered her a ride to the store the other day when she was waiting for the bus, but she turned me down. She seems so sad. I've tried to reach out to her, but she hasn't wanted to even talk."

"Keep trying," suggested Kate. "Maybe she'll stick around and eventually be willing to accept the help."

Abby signed, "all done" and Joe washed her hands and set her on the floor. Grace had fallen asleep in the playpen, so the adults lingered over coffee. Abby came into the kitchen with her favorite toy from grandma's toy box. It was a dollhouse that had furniture and a family that all fit inside the house. There was a handle to carry the house and a latch to make sure the house stayed closed, so everything didn't fall out when it was carried. It was the latch that was giving Abby trouble. She half carried half dragged the dollhouse to Charlie. Setting it down, she looked at Charlie and signed "help, please." Charlie opened the latch and all the adults watched to see what Abby's next move would be. They knew if she tried to take it back to the living room with it opened everything would spill out. Apparently, Abby knew that too. She sat down by Charlie's chair and started playing.

Kate had called her mom as soon as they got the news that Grace could hear. Ruth asked if this news changed their minds about having more children. Kate said that for now, they would continue on the path toward adoption.

They felt the Lord calling them to adopt and that maybe Grace failing her newborn hearing test was God's way of nudging them in that direction. Ruth and Charlie were silent for a moment and then Charlie promised they would continue to pray the Lord will bring the right children to their home.

Kate stood then and said, 'let's get the dishes done so we can get Abby home and in bed."

"Don't worry about it," said Ruth. "Charlie and I have a system. We will do them after you leave."

"Are you sure?" asked Kate.

"We're sure," answered Ruth.

Joe told Abby it was time to go and helped her to pick up the dollhouse pieces and redo the latch. Together they carried it into the living room and put it away. Soon the family was out the door and headed home.

Later as Kate and Joe relaxed before bed, they talked about their desire to have their son home for Christmas. Kate said, "If Cheryl hadn't sped up our classes, we wouldn't even be talking about our son coming home." They decided they would pray specifically that God would send them a son before Christmas if that was his will for them. They also decided they needed to pray for patience. They were quiet for a few minutes each busy with their own thoughts.

Saturday night as they were preparing for bed, Joe said, "I think we need to plan to get those clothes for the boys put away tomorrow during the girls' naps."

"I agree," said Kate. "Do you think we could stop on the way home from church and pick up a few plastic bins to store them in?"

Joe asked, "you don't want to put them in the dressers?"

"I thought about that," Kate said, "but if I put them in the bins, it will be easier to store what we don't need when we get a call. I know that we will probably have at least a few weeks of visitation with our son in his foster home before bringing him home. But I want to be prepared in case the agency calls with an at-risk placement. If that happens, we won't have much warning."

Joe agreed with her reasoning and said, "I'll plan on stopping." Shortly after, the couple headed to bed.

22

Sunday morning things did not go well. Joe was supposed to be there 20 minutes before service to pray with the pastor and then to be available to greet people. Joe was trying to dress Abby who was giving him a tough time. He was trying to help her put on the purple dress Kate had laid out for her.

She kept signing, "no, want pink dress." She was getting very upset. Since it was getting late, he checked with Kate to see if there was a reason, she wanted the purple dress on Abby or if she could wear a pink one.

"Since she has white tights on pink is fine," Kate answered.

Relieved Joe went back to Abby's room and opened the closet door. He bent down and signed and said, "what dress, show me?" Abby looked in the closet and started to cry.

She kept signing "pink dress." Kate had finished dressing Grace and came to see if she could help. Handing Grace to her daddy, she tried to figure out why their normally so complacent daughter was so upset. She pulled out three pink dresses and offered them to Abby.

Abby signed, "no, no, no."

Kate signed, "show me" and picked her up and held her level with the dresses hanging in the closet.

Abby signed, "no here."

Kate knew there were no dresses in the laundry and was about to admit defeat when understanding dawned on her. Setting Abby down Kate signed, "come" and led Abby to the Noah's ark room.

As soon as she entered the room Abby ran to the bed. and grabbed her new pink dress. and signed, "pink dress" with a huge grin on her face.

Finally ready and only 5 minutes behind Joe took Abby out to the car while Kate picked Grace up from the playpen where Joe had put her while he packed the diaper bag and Kate dealt with Abby. Just as Kate picked up Grace, she spit up on her outfit and Kate's blouse. Oh no, not this morning when we are already late, Kate thought. She quickly changed Grace and was buckling her into her car seat when Joe stuck his head in the door to find out what was keeping Kate. She handed the car seat to Joe with a quick explanation and raced back to her room to change her blouse. When they were finally on their way, they were now almost 15 minutes late.

Seeing the tension on her face, Joe said, "relax everyone will understand. And besides," he joked, "since we are usually there 20 minutes before service, we should still be 5 minutes early and beat the majority of the church family." Knowing he was right and that worrying wouldn't change anything, she relaxed and smiled.

"We have a hard time with two. What will happen when we add another child or two?"

"We will trust God and do our best," Joe reminded her. Believing the truth of his words, Kate felt the peace of God flood her soul.

As Joe pulled into the parking lot six minutes before the start of service, he turned to Kate and said, "we didn't forget something did we?" The parking lot was full of cars. More cars than for a normal Sunday morning and it was still not even time for the service to begin, Puzzled, he parked the car and unhooked Grace's car seat while Kate got Abby out of the car. They quickly entered the church and were surprised to find no one in sight. Something was going on. The foyer never cleared before the middle of the first song, and it hadn't even started yet. Cautiously they went towards the sanctuary. Pastor Alan stood at the front of the sanctuary surrounded by three toy boxes filled with boys' toys. Each box appeared to hold toys appropriate for a certain age. The first box appeared to have toys for a two- or three-year-old, the second box for a four-year-old, and the third box maybe a five- or six-year-old. When the pastor spotted Joe and Kate, he motioned to the people, and they all started singing "Jesus loves the little children." When they finished, Pastor Alan called Joe and Kate to the front of the room. He explained that their willingness to adopt was a ministry and the church wanted to be sure they had everything they needed to do the job. They knew they had no toys for little boys in their home. So, the church family decided to get them some. The pastor teased Joe and Kate that they sure made the surprise easier to pull off by arriving late. The whole congregation joined in laughter. When everyone was again quiet Pastor Alan led the congregation in prayer asking God to bring the children, he wanted into the Kanell family in his time. Kate and Joe thanked everyone, and people settled down for service.

Joe and Kate were still so overwhelmed by the generosity

of the church family that they forgot to stop for bins on the way home. After lunch, Joe settled Abby down for her nap. They had made some strides over the last few months, and she was able to close her eyes for sleep much better. While he was getting Abby down for her nap, Kate was feeding Grace and getting her tucked in for a nap. They finished about the same time and met in the Noah's ark room. Kate and Joe looked at each other and at the same time said, "We forgot the bins."

They laughed and Joe said, "I'll go grab some bins."

When Joe returned, he asked, "Do you want my help, or should I bring up the toy boxes?

"Go ahead and bring up the toy boxes," she said. "I don't think this will take too long." She decided to leave the smallest clothes in the Noah's ark room. She would put the largest clothes in the green jungle room. The middle-size clothes would go in the blue car room. When Joe came up with the first toy box, she directed him to the appropriate room. As she suspected she was soon done with the clothes and joined Joe in looking through the toy boxes. As they finished looking through the last toy box Kate turned to Joe and said, "this is Biblical, isn't it?"

Joe looked at her and said, "what do you mean?"

She responded with, "Philippians 4:19"

And my God will meet all your needs according to the riches of his glory in Christ Jesus.

"Everything - the house, the gift from Uncle Herb that allowed us to get the furniture and the clothes, the help from the church family with the move, and now this, toys for sons we don't even know. It's amazing. And now we wait for what God has for us next." They finished up getting the rooms ready. Now the rooms, the house, and

Kate and Joe themselves were ready to meet their new son. Now they waited. Joe went to go over his notes for youth group that evening. Kate peeked in on Abby and Grace and seeing they were still asleep, she curled up on the bed with an afghan over her and started thinking over all that had happened in the past 3 months. It wasn't long before she drifted off to sleep.

She woke with a start and glanced at the clock. She was amazed to see it was 4:30. She listened carefully and could hear Joe in the kitchen with Abby and Grace. Joe was so good to her. She stretched and sat up. Sliding her feet into her slippers, she went into the bathroom, washed her face, and brushed her hair.

She then went down to the kitchen where Joe had their traditional Sunday night grilled cheese and tomato soup started. She came up behind him and wrapped her arms around his waist. "Thanks," she said. She loosened her hold as she felt him turning around. When they were facing each other, he bent down and kissed her.

"Did you sleep well?" Joe asked.

"I did," she answered. "Thanks again, I must have been more tired than I thought. I didn't even hear the girls. How long have they been up?"

Joe glanced at the clock before he answered. "Abby's been up for about an hour. Grace's been up for about 10 minutes. I didn't even get her changed because I was in the middle of starting dinner. If you want to change her and feed her, I'll finish cooking dinner," Joe offered.

Kate agreeing to the plan picked up Grace and headed to the bedroom. When Kate returned a short while later, with a contented Grace who had her belly full and a dry diaper, she found Abby munching happily on her grilled

141

cheese sandwich. Joe looked up apologetically; "she was hungry, so I let her start,"

"That was a good idea," Kate said. "Maybe we can actually get to church on time tonight?"

Joe laughed as he set Kate's plate and bowl on the table. He then grabbed his bowl and plate from the counter and joined Kate at the table. They bowed their heads for prayer and started eating. There was little conversation as they both knew they needed to hurry a little or they would be late for church twice in one day.

OCTOBER 3, 2011

Monday morning Kate was awake before Joe. She prayed and asked God for his peace. She reminded herself who was in control, and she did feel God's peace. Cheryl was coming this morning to do their home inspection. After breakfast, she debated sending Abby to pick out a book but opted not to start a book. Abby did not like to stop in the middle and because they had to sign all the pictures as well as the words, books could take a while. Instead, she got out Abby's puzzles. If Cheryl arrived before Abby finished, she was able to continue independently. When Cheryl arrived, Abby kept signing "come" and "see." Kate and Joe had no idea what she wanted to show Cheryl. Cheryl good-naturedly took Abby's hand and let her lead her up the stairs. Kate was surprised when Abby took Cheryl into the blue car room.

When Cheryl went into the first of the boy's rooms, she looked at Joe and Kate quizzically. "Do you know something I don't?"

Kate laughed a little nervously and explained how they had stopped at the mall on Monday to get some clothes for the girls. She explained about the clearance sales and that they had decided to pick up a few items to be prepared.

"And the toys?" Cheryl asked.

Joe explained how the church had surprised them the day before. Cheryl looked at the rest of the bedrooms and then turned to Joe and Kate, "once you sign your home study you will then be ready to start sending it to agencies that have little boys available for adoption."

Tuesday evening Ruth called and told Kate that the quiet lady from unit one left on Monday morning without saying a word. Ruth said, "I saw her get on the bus on Monday and had called a greeting. She didn't have a suitcase or anything, but she hasn't returned. Since she hasn't paid for this week, I assume she won't be back. We had a call from a family that needs a place starting tomorrow. Since that's the only available unit I need to get in there and clean it out in the morning. If she has left items behind, I'll box them and save them for 30 days. Since we don't require identification, I'm not even sure she gave us her real name. She wasn't sent by social services and always paid in cash. I never did get her to talk to me. I'll add her to my prayer list. The new family has two little girls about the ages of your two. Their home was damaged by fire, but not destroyed. They had insurance and will be able to get the damage repaired. but they needed a place to stay until it was ready. They had already checked into a hotel for tonight, but since it could take weeks to finish their home social services sent them our way." They talked for a few more minutes. They hung up with plans for Ruth and Charlie to join Kate's family for dinner Wednesday night.

24

TUESDAY

The little boy sat silently in the dark closet, tears rolling down his cheeks. He wore nothing but a pair of underwear. He had to go to the bathroom, but the closet was locked. He had already wet himself, but it was dry now and he hoped She wouldn't notice. If She didn't come back soon, he knew his body would force him to wet himself again. He also knew that if he did, She would beat him. Again. The effort to keep from wetting himself hurt so bad, that he wondered if it was worth it to keep trying. But She might come back any minute and if he could just wait her out, maybe he could avoid a beating. Maybe. But then She seemed to like beating him. Finally, his body took over and he was forced to relieve himself. The relief allowed him to consider his situation. She always locked him in this closet when she left their rooms. Sometimes She left him a bottle of water and some crackers. She had this time, but they were gone. She didn't usually leave for so long. It had been light out when she left. The closet door had cracks where he could see a little light. When it got dark last night, he thought She would come. But She didn't.

Now it was morning again. Surely, She would come today. He spent the day dozing and waking. It was hard to get comfortable in the small closet even though he wasn't very big. He was hungry and thirsty and that made it hard for him to sleep. His arm hurt from where She had squeezed it so hard when She put him in the closet. When he saw the light fading through the cracks, he knew night was coming again. Daddy his heart cried out where are you? When you went to the war, you promised you'd come back to me and mommy. We need you, daddy. Mommy says you went to see Jesus. Aren't you done seeing him yet? I need you, daddy. Mommy got so sad about you seeing Jesus that she kept taking medicine and sometimes she even took shots. Now she has left me, too. I tried asking Jesus to send you back, but he didn't. I'm scared, daddy. And hungry. And thirsty. And my arm hurts. If you can't come back to me, can you maybe ask Jesus if I can come to see him too? Then he remembered his mommy and daddy telling him he could always pray when he was scared. So, he closed his eyes and prayed, dear Jesus I need my daddy. Can you please send him back to me? If that's not okay, can I please come to your house and be with my daddy? Amen. He felt a little better and tried to sleep some more. The next time he opened his eyes he could see the sun through the cracks. He listened carefully to see if he heard She. He knew what he was supposed to call her but refused to think of her as anything other than She. Unless it was She Monster. But he didn't hear anything. When she was sleeping, She usually snored and even though he listened really hard he didn't hear anything. He tried the door in case She had come back and unlocked it. It was still locked. It was easier to sleep now, and he was glad he hadn't needed to use the bathroom for a while. Maybe when She did come back, She wouldn't notice that he had wet. He dozed back off for a little longer. He woke slowly. It was too hard to move. He tried to figure out what woke him and then realized he heard voices. It wasn't She, but he could hear two people talking. He listened carefully. A man was talking. Could it be daddy? No, this man didn't sound anything like daddy. He heard the man say, "what smells so bad?"

The lady said, "it seems to be coming from here. Charlie, when did you put a lock on this closet?"

The man answered, "I never put a lock on the closet. I'll go get something to cut it off." The boy dozed off again. It was so hard to stay awake. He was barely aware of the man returning.

He tried to rouse himself when the door swung open and he heard the woman say, "Oh, Charlie, it's a child. Call 911."

Charlie called 911. While they waited for the ambulance and police to arrive, Charlie called Kate and explained, that an emergency has come up at the motel with a child in one of the units and the situation needs prayer. I'll call and explain later. Bye. While Charlie was on the phone with Kate, Ruth had been praying quietly but aloud for this small child. Charlie hung up the phone and told Ruth, as soon as possible you had better call and reassure Kate.

Ruth gave a one-sided grin and replied, "I'm sure Kate didn't like not knowing all the details." Ruth looked into the cupboard and saw that the child's eyes were open. She couldn't tell for sure, but she thought it was a little boy. She smiled and said, "you can come out, nobody will hurt you." He tried to move but it hurt too much and was just too hard, so he just stayed where he was. Ruth turned to Charlie and asked him, "do you think we should lift him out?"

"I don't know," Charlie answered. "I don't want to hurt him." Just then they heard the sirens. The police and paramedics would be here in a minute. Charlie went out to wave the ambulance over to the right door. While the police talked to Charlie outside the door, Ruth gave what little information she could to the paramedic.

The paramedic said, "if he's been in here since Monday his biggest problem is going to be dehydration. I'll get an IV started right away and get some fluid into him. That one arm is bruised, and he has a lot of black and blue marks, but I don't see enough bruising to suggest internal injuries. I'm going to lift him out so I can better assess his status." The paramedic lifted out the small child. Ruth had been right it was a little boy. As the paramedic lifted him out of the closet, his eyes remained fixed on Ruth. Seeing this the paramedic asked, "do you know him?"

"No," Ruth said, "the woman, Jane Jones, who rented this unit claimed it was just her."

"Well," the paramedic responded, "he seems to trust you.:

Charlie came back into the room and said, "Ruth, the police want to talk to you now."

Ruth turned to the little boy and said, "I'll be right back." When she started to leave, the little boy started to panic, and become very agitated, yet he still didn't make a sound.

"Wait," called the paramedic. "We need to keep him as still and calm as possible while we try to stabilize him enough to transfer him to the hospital." Ruth turned back while Charlie went to explain to the officer.

Charlie returned and said, "the officer said do whatever you have to help that little boy. He said he has a son about that age and can't believe what has happened here." Ruth reached out and gently touched the back of the little boy's hand with one finger. His hand moved slightly, and Ruth was going to move her hand when he weakly wrapped his small fingers around her finger. She allowed her hand to stay in his.

The paramedic was trying to get an IV started and Ruth heard him mutter, "his veins are so small because he is so dehydrated." Finally, on the fifth try, he was able to get it started. Ruth felt like crying with relief. Through it all the little boy had not made a sound.

With the IV established the paramedic said, "let's get him to the hospital where they can check the extent of his injuries." Since he still clung weakly to her finger Ruth followed the stretcher to the ambulance. When she let go, so they could lift the stretcher into the ambulance his eyes stayed glued on Ruth. When they tried to shut the ambulance door he started to flail. The paramedic quickly opened the door and called to Ruth, "hey would you mind riding along? I'd feel much better if we can keep him quiet until we can get him to the hospital."

She looked at Charlie who said, "I'll follow the ambulance."

Then she looked at the officer who said, "I'll see you at the hospital."

Ruth turned and climbed into the ambulance. The paramedic pointed to a place where Ruth could sit. The little boy could see her without her being in the way.

25

The ride to the hospital took about ten minutes. The driver must have radioed ahead about the boy's attachment to Ruth because the doctors at the hospital had Ruth come into the examining room with him. When the technicians brought in the portable X-ray machine, Ruth stood outside the room where he could see her through the window. After about an hour the doctor motioned Ruth out of the room. They stood where the boy could see Ruth, but not hear them talking. The doctor said, "he has bruising consistent with abuse. His left arm has a small hairline fracture about an inch above the wrist, but the bone is still in alignment. I'm going to cast as a precaution. He is severely dehydrated but is responding well to fluids. Social Services has been alerted and will be here soon. If we can get him to eat and drink something, I'll discharge him this afternoon."

Ruth said, "I'd be glad to try and get him to eat."

"Not too much," the doctor cautioned. "He may try to eat too much too fast and end up sick. The nurse will bring some pudding and apple juice as soon as I finish putting the cast on his arm. See if he'll take three or four bites of the pudding and about an ounce of the juice. If that stays down, he can have a little more every fifteen minutes or so." Ruth went back into the room and held the boy's hand while the doctor put a bright blue cast on his arm. The doctor talked to the boy while he worked telling him, "this will keep your arm from getting hurt worse if you bump it. You will have it on for about four to six weeks and then your arm will be better." As soon as the doctor finished, the nurse brought in the pudding and juice. The boy's eyes lit up when he saw the pudding and juice.

The nurse laughed seeing his expression and said to Ruth, "I don't think you are going to have a problem getting him to take three or four bites. I think the problem is going to be to get him to take only three or four bites."

They laughed together and turning to the little boy Ruth said, "ok, Buddy, I have some pudding for you and a little juice. It has been a few days since you ate. If you eat all of this at once, your tummy might get sick. You can eat it all but a little at a time. Do you understand?" She was thrilled to see him nod his head yes. It was the first response they had gotten from him all day. Ruth knew the doctor was concerned that he had yet to utter a sound. He obviously understood but either couldn't or wouldn't talk. He ate his four bites and drank a little juice and watched carefully as Ruth left them on the cabinet by the bed.

"Do you know how old you are?" Ruth asked. She was thrilled to see him hold up three fingers. "You're three years old?" Ruth asked. He nodded his head yes. "Do you know your name?" was Ruth's next question. Again, the boy nodded. "Can you tell me?" Ruth asked. She waited, seeing the struggle on his face. Slowly he shook his head no. "That's okay," Ruth assured him. "How about I call you Buddy? Would that be okay?" With a relieved look on his face, he nodded yes.

That afternoon Kate waited impatiently for her parents to call back. They still hadn't called as she came downstairs from settling the kids for their naps. Since getting her hearing aids Abby slept much better. As she was debating calling her mom, the phone rang. She grabbed the phone expecting it to be her mom. Her heart skipped a beat when she saw Cheryl's number.

"Your home study is ready to sign, and I may have a boy for you. Can I come over now to have you sign it? As soon as it's signed, I can tell you about the little boy."

During the fifteen minutes that it took Cheryl to arrive Kate couldn't sit still. She completely forgot about calling her mother. Joe wasn't much better.

Cheryl finally arrived. Just as she walked in the door her phone rang. Fortunately, it was a short call. "First things first. I need you to sign this." When the forms were signed, Cheryl said, "I have been assured that the child that was found abandoned isn't listed as missing." She went on to explain the child's situation. Joe and Kate readily agreed. They agreed to meet in an hour to pick up their new son. Cheryl explained, "usually the agency will bring the child to you. However, the police took him to the hospital, and we feel it would be less traumatic for him if you pick him up and take him home than if I pick him up and then leave him at your house." Joe and Kate agreed with the reasoning.

Before Cheryl left, they phoned Jenny and asked if she could take both girls for a little while. Jenny agreed but hearing the excitement in her friend's voice demanded, "what's up?"

Kate laughed and said, "we need to go pick up our son. I'll fill you in later."

When Kate hung up the phone, Cheryl asked, "was that Jenny?" When Kate confirmed it was, Cheryl laughed and responded, "I'm surprised you got away without a full explanation."

Kate joined in the laughter and said, "she did threaten to die of curiosity before we got there. I'm sure she'll demand a few more details."

Over the next hour, Buddy finished the pudding and the juice. Ruth was about to ring for the nurse when Cheryl from Social Services entered the hospital room. She identified herself and asked to talk to Ruth. When Buddy started to panic as they walked towards the door, Ruth turned and said, "I'll be right outside the door just like before." He settled back on the bed but kept a close watch on Ruth who had positioned herself so Buddy could see her through the window.

Cheryl had some questions for Ruth. "Do you think the woman who registered at the motel was his mother?"

"I'm not sure," answered Ruth. "If she was, why did she hide him? We don't charge extra for a child."

Cheryl thought for a minute and said, "that makes sense. However, he doesn't match anyone in our database of missing children. Has he talked at all?" was Cheryl's next question.

"No," Ruth answered, "not even a whimper."

"I think that is all the questions I have for now," said Cheryl. "I have found him a home. If the woman at the motel is indeed his mother, he will most likely be freed for adoption. If we get him freed for adoption, this family will adopt him."

"That would be great," said Ruth.

Cheryl looked uncomfortable and taking a deep breath

said, "I want to thank you for taking the time to come to the hospital and for all you've done for this little boy. However, I need to ask you to do something hard. I need you to say goodbye and walk away. He has attached himself to you in a short time, which shows he can attach and bond to new adults. His trust hasn't been completely shattered. My fear is if you are still here when the foster parents arrive, he will cling to you and not want to go with them. They should be here in about ten minutes."

"Can I tell him he is going to a new family?" asked Ruth.

"Yes," Cheryl said, "just don't promise him you will see him again. If you want, I can give your name and number to the foster parents in case they have any questions. They may feel contact with you might be a good closure or they might feel it would open old wounds. I'll leave that up to them.

Do you have a way home?" Cheryl asked. "I understand you came in the ambulance."

"Yes," Ruth responded, "my husband is waiting with the officer who still needs to question me."

"OK," Cheryl continued, "if you will tell him goodbye quickly, the foster parents should be here soon."

Ruth blinked back her tears, swallowed the lump in her throat, and put a smile on her face. Buddy was such a sweet little boy and had so quickly found a place in her heart. As much as she didn't want it to, what Cheryl said about her need to leave made sense. She pushed open the door and went and sat on Buddy's bed. She looked over her shoulder and saw that Cheryl was standing by the door. "Buddy," Ruth began praying for wisdom, "this is my new friend Cheryl. She has a new family for you. A family that will give you food and clothes. They will never ever lock you in a closet. They will be your new mommy and daddy. You will be safe. I have to go now. The officer needs to talk to me. Cheryl will stay with you." Ruth turned to look at her.

Cheryl took her cue and moved toward the bed. "Yes, Buddy I will stay right here until you leave with your new mommy and your new daddy," Cheryl said. "After Ruth leaves, I can tell you about your new home."

Ruth hugged Buddy and said, "have fun in your new home." Buddy clung tightly to her. She didn't want to force him to let go so she said, "let's ask Cheryl if you will have any brothers and sisters." Buddy let go and turned to Cheryl.

Ruth slipped out the door as Cheryl took over explaining about Buddy's new family. Cheryl made a mental note to send a thank you to Ruth. That had gone so much smoother than she anticipated.

Ruth headed down the hall to the lobby to find Charlie and the officer. She went straight into Charlie's arms and sobbed. He held her for a long moment. When she had herself in reasonable control, she said, "the department of social services has found him a foster home that hopes to adopt him. Cheryl, the worker, felt he would attach to them better if I had already left. They will be here any minute."

The officer spoke, "I have arranged to use a room to take your statement. If you are ready, we can go there now. It's right this way." Ruth and Charlie followed him down the hall. They entered a room about halfway down the hall. As the door closed behind them, the door into the lobby opened, and in walked Buddy's foster parents. Josiah and Kate Kanell.

26

Kate and Joe walked up to the desk and Joe said, "my name is Josiah Kanell and I'm looking for Cheryl from social services."

The receptionist looked up and smiled. "Cheryl said you were coming." She gave them directions on where to find Cheryl and they went down the hall to meet their new son.

When they got to the room, they stood outside looking in the window. "Oh Joe," Kate whispered, "he's beautiful." Joe looked at the small boy in the big bed. He was filthy except for the casted arm. His hair appeared to be blond but was so matted and dirty he couldn't tell for sure. At that moment Buddy looked up and spotted Joe and Kate looking in. His face clearly showed his terror. Kate's and Joe's hearts went out to the small boy.

Seeing the terror on Buddy's face Cheryl turned and saw Joe and Kate. She called them into the room and said, "this is Joe and Kate. You are going to go live with them."

Kate knelt so she was on eye level with Buddy. She spoke to him quietly trying to not scare him anymore. She said, "Hi Buddy. My name is Kate. You can call me Kate if you want, but I want to be your mommy and I hope you will be able to call me mommy. At our house, we have a little girl who can't hear or talk. She talks with her hands. You can learn to talk with your hands too. Then you can tell us what you want. Would you like that?" He nodded yes. "Ok," Kate continued. "We are going to start with two right now. Do you want to call me Kate?" she asked? He shook his head no. "Do you want to call me mommy?" He nodded his head. She showed him the sign for mommy and told him what it meant. He copied her movements. His eyes went immediately to Joe. "Do you want to learn the sign for daddy?" Another nod.

Joe squatted down to be closer to Buddy's level. He signed and said, "daddy." Buddy copied him. "Since we don't know your name can we call you Buddy?" He nodded his head. Kate got up off the floor and pulled a chair near the bed. "Would you like to come sit on my lap?" Kate asked Buddy. Buddy looked at Kate, then at Joe thinking. Then he slowly held out his arms to be picked up.

As Kate carefully picked up her new son, Joe whispered, "thank you, Jesus." When Buddy heard what Joe said, he sighed and leaned back against Kate.

Cheryl who had been watching the scene unfold, said, "I'll get him discharged and you can go home."

Twenty minutes later still in the hospital gown, Buddy was buckled into a new car seat the agency had provided and they were heading home. Joe asked Kate, "do you want to stop and get the girls or go home first and I can go back and get them.?

Kate thought and then responded, "I think home first would be best."

"I agree," said Joe and headed for home. Up until now, Kate had dealt with Buddy. She had carried him to the car and buckled him in. Now Joe wanted a chance to hold their new son. When the car stopped, Joe opened Buddy's door and unbuckled his car seat straps. Then he held out his arms and waited. He didn't have to wait very long. Buddy hesitated only a few seconds before he held out his arms to Joe. Joe gently picked up his son and carried him into the house. The hospital had warned them that Buddy would be weak for a few days, and they shouldn't require very much effort from him. Because of this, Joe continued to carry Buddy through the house showing him around. When they got upstairs, Joe stopped first at the green safari room. Buddy looked in with interest. When they got to the blue car room his face lit up with a smile.

Kate seeing the smile said, "Buddy this is your room." He looked at her with wonder and pointed to himself.

Joe said, "yes Buddy, just for you."

"Now," Kate said, "how about I give you a bath and we get you out of the hospital clothes and into your new clothes?" Buddy looked a little uncertain but nodded his head yes. Kate asked, "Joe will you put the bin of size three clothes into Buddy's room?"

Joe answered, "sure and then I'll go get the girls before Grace gets too hungry."

Kate took Buddy into her arms and carried him into the bathroom. She wrapped his cast with the plastic wrap she had grabbed when they came through the kitchen to keep it dry. She filled the tub with warm water and gently set Buddy in the water. She washed him and shampooed his hair. After she finished rinsing him off, Kate lifted him out and wrapped him in a big towel. She pulled the plug to let the tub drain and picking up Buddy, she carried him to his bedroom. Kate stood Buddy on the floor next to the bed to finish drying him off. She pulled a pair of underwear out of the bin and helped Buddy put them on. She lifted him onto the bed and gave him a choice of a red shirt with cars or a blue shirt with dinosaurs. He picked the red one. Kate helped him get the shirt over his cast and then slipped him into a pair of new jeans.

She carried Buddy over to the toy box. "These are your toys, Buddy," Kate said. "Would you like to pick one out to play with?" Buddy looked in the toy box with curiosity and spotting a bulldozer and dump truck he smiled and pointed to them. Kate pulled the dump truck out of the box and handed it to Buddy. She then pulled out the bulldozer and gave that to him also. Grabbing the wet towel, she picked up her son and his new toys and went downstairs. She set the little boy and his toys on the kitchen floor. Opening a door off the kitchen that led to the laundry room, Kate tossed the towel into the hamper.

Going to the cupboard she took out a sippy cup and put about two ounces of milk in the cup. She handed it to Buddy and said, "we have lots of food, but the doctor said only a little at a time." He nodded and took the cup. Kate started making half of a peanut butter and jelly sandwich. When she was done, she set Buddy up at the table and gave him the sandwich. She checked his cup and seeing it was empty she gave him a little more. He ate the sandwich and finished the milk.

She could see he was very tired, so she said, "time for a nap." She hoped he wouldn't fight her on it. She picked him up and he laid his head on her shoulder. All the way upstairs she debated the wisdom of rocking him or just laying him down on the bed. Checking the time, she decided to just lay him down. Joe should be home soon with Abby and a very hungry Grace. She tucked him into his bed and said he could meet Abby and Grace after his nap. She promised that Mommy and Daddy would be there when he woke up. He curled up in a little ball in the bed.

Kate prayed, "Dear Jesus thank you for Buddy. Help him sleep well. Amen." He sighed and drifted off to sleep. As he drifted off to sleep, Kate heard Joe come into the kitchen with the girls. Grace was fussing and Kate knew that the fussing would soon turn to full-out cries if she didn't get fed soon. She took a last look at her sleeping son and went to feed her daughter.

As Kate settled into the rocking chair in the living room to nurse Grace, Abby was running from room to room. She finally came back to stand in front of Kate and signed "where" and "boy."

Kate signed and said "sleeping,"

Abby responded, "Abby go"?

Kate quickly signed and said, "no, go Daddy come". Abby knew "go daddy come" meant she had to go to Daddy and get him to come to mommy. She quickly obeyed and went running in search of Joe. Kate could hear him in the kitchen, so she knew Abby wouldn't have any trouble finding him. When Abby came back with Joe, Kate had just raised Grace to her shoulder for a burp. As Kate patted Grace's little back, she explained that Abby wanted to see her new brother.

Joe said, "I'll take Abby up and let her see Buddy. I want to check on him anyway."

"Thanks," Kate said. Kate listened but didn't hear Joe's voice, so she assumed that Buddy was still asleep, and he was signing only to Abby. Her suspicions were confirmed when Joe and Abby came back downstairs a few minutes later.

Abby ran up to Kate and signed, "B boy sleep car room."

"Yes," Kate said, "Buddy is sleeping in the car room."

Abby signed, "play later?"

"Yes," said Joe, "Buddy and Abby can play later."

Grace was done eating so Kate changed her and tucked her in for a nap.

When she came downstairs, she asked Joe, "did Abby sleep at Jenny's?"

Joe responded, "she slept for about an hour." Joe's plan this morning had to be to go to his office at the church right after the kids went down for their naps. Now he was torn. He had things to do at the church, but he wanted to be here when Buddy woke up.

As if reading his mind, Kate asked, "are you going to the church?"

Joe laughed and said, "that is exactly what I'm asking myself. I know if I call Pastor Alan and explain he'll tell me to stay home. With all the time off around our move, I'm a little behind and I don't want to shirk my responsibility. What do we have planned for this weekend?" Joe asked.

Kate said, "nothing on Saturday. Nate, Jenny, and the kids are coming home with us after church."

Joe thought for a minute and then said, "would it work for you if I put in about 4 hours at the church on Saturday?"

"I don't see any problem with that," Kate answered.

"That's what I'll do then," said Joe. "Let me check if that works for Pastor Alan." Joe went to call Pastor Alan and Kate went to check on Buddy. When Kate got upstairs Buddy was still asleep. She stood gazing at the beautiful little boy who was their son. His too-long blond hair was clean and combed. It curled a little on the ends as he slept.

She knew his eyes were blue. She prayed and thanked God for this child. She had only known he existed for less than a day, and still, her heart was filled with love for him.

As she stood watching him sleep Joe came up behind her with his laptop computer. "I can sit in his room and work," he said. "Then when he wakes up, he'll be able to see someone immediately."

"Thanks," Kate said, "I'll go get dinner started."

About an hour later Joe came downstairs carrying Buddy. When Abby spotted them, she began to dance around signing, "hi B boy."

Buddy looked at Joe questioningly. Joe said, "she's saying hi to you." He stood Buddy on his feet near Abby. Squatting down he started to sign and talk saying, "Buddy this is Abby. She can't hear very well. Her hearing aids help her hear. She hasn't learned to talk with her mouth yet. She is learning to talk with her fingers. Remember when we showed you the signs for mommy and daddy?"

Buddy nodded and signed "daddy" and then pointed to Joe.

"That's right you remember," Joe praised him. "Abby is excited you are here to be her brother. We also have a baby named Grace. She is taking a nap right now." Buddy covered his ears and pointed to the stairs. Joe looked puzzled for a minute, then understanding dawned on him. "Are you asking if baby Grace can hear?" Joe asked. Buddy smiled and nodded his head. "Grace can hear," said Joe.

Kate can into the room and said, "dinner is in the oven and will be ready in about 20 minutes. My dad called and said mom has a headache and postponed dinner until tomorrow night."

Joe responded, "it's probably better if we keep things quiet for tonight. Did you tell them?"

"No," she grinned, "I thought it would make a nice surprise."

Buddy signed "mommy" and pointed to Kate, then looked at Joe.

"Yes, Buddy that's mommy and you did the sign just right."

Abby signed "come puzzle" to Buddy.

He looked to Joe. Joe translated demonstrating each sign. "This is the sign for come and this is puzzle. Abby wants you to play with her puzzles. If you want to play with Abby, this is the sign for yes."

Buddy turned to Abby and signed "yes". The two children played happily until it was time for dinner.

Kate had gone to the kitchen to check on the macaroni and cheese she had in the oven. Seeing that it was done she called to Joe, "it's time to eat."

Buddy gently touched Abby's arm so she would look at him and signed "come". They both stood up and Buddy took her hand and led her to the kitchen. Joe was so touched he had to swallow the lump in his throat before he could follow the kids. Kate saw his look and raised an eyebrow. He mouthed later.

During supper, Buddy saw Abby sign "more" and "please" and get more macaroni and cheese. When he was done, he signed "more" and "please."

Kate asked if he wanted more, and he signed yes. She gave him some more.

Just as Kate was serving the chocolate pudding for

dessert, she heard Grace. "I'll go get her," Kate said. Turning to Buddy, she said, "finish your pudding, and then you can meet Grace."

By the time she came back downstairs with Grace, Joe and the kids had finished eating and cleared up supper. They were in the living room. Buddy was pointing to one thing after another and then looking at Joe. Joe would sign it. Buddy would repeat the sign and look to Joe to check if he had done it right. Then Buddy would point to the object and sign it for Abby. Abby played along for about ten minutes and then tired of the game. Buddy continued for a little longer then walked over and stood in front of Joe. Joe held out his arms and Buddy went right into them. Joe picked him up and cuddled him close. It wasn't long before Abby climbed into her mother's lap and cuddled down next to Grace. Kate and Joe enjoyed cuddling their children, but after a few minutes, they decided to start getting them ready for bed. The older two were getting tired. Buddy and Abby settled down quickly and were soon asleep. Joe decided to do a little more church work at the desk in their room to be close to the kids.

Kate went downstairs, taking Grace with her. She put Grace in the playpen and started a load of laundry. Since Grace was playing happily, she decided to make a batch of brownies for dessert for the next night. She wasn't sure what the next day might look like. She knew that Joe had to be at the church most of the day. She slipped the pan of brownies into the oven. As she set the timer, she grinned. Jenny's kids would be in bed in about ten minutes. She expected a call from Jenny within five minutes after that.

She started loading the dishwasher with the dishes Joe and the kids had stacked in the sink as well as her baking dishes. She was just finishing when the timer went off for the brownies. As she turned off the timer, she realized she hadn't heard from Jenny. As soon as she got Grace into her pajamas, she would call. She set the brownies to cool and was picking up Grace when the backdoor opened and in came Jenny. Kate laughed. "I was expecting a call. I figured you would be dying of curiosity."

Jenny joined in her laughter. "A phone call wouldn't do. I had to see him. What did your parents think when they came for supper?"

Kate said, "Mom had a headache and we postponed until tomorrow. I decided to surprise them."

"Where is he?" demanded Jenny.

"Sleeping," Kate said. "Come along and you can peek at him while I get Grace ready for bed." Kate and Jenny started up the stairs.

Joe stuck his head out the bedroom door and teased, "nice restraint Jenny. I figured you'd beg Nate to let you come over right after dinner."

"That was my plan," laughed Jenny, "but he was late getting home from work. I left as soon as he came in the door so I can't stay long. Which room is he in?"

"The car room," answered Kate.

Jenny looked into the room and exclaimed, he's adorable!" She followed Kate into Grace's room and asked, "what's his name?"

"We don't know," Kate said. "He was found abandoned and either can't or won't talk. We've been calling him Buddy."

"Do you know how old he is?"

"Not for sure. When we asked him, he held up three fingers, but he acts older. He reminds me of Sammy, especially with how he treats Abby." She told Jenny about Buddy bringing Abby to supper.

"I can't wait to meet him," Jenny said. "Do you still want us to come for dinner on Sunday?"

"Of course," Kate said. "If he's going to be part of this family, he is going to have to meet the whole family. Joe and I haven't talked about church on Sunday yet. He's still weak, but he's got three full days before Sunday. We'll have to wait and see."

Jenny said, "I've got to run, we'll see you Sunday then."

28

Buddy slept through the night. Kate had checked on him twice during the night, but he seemed to be sleeping peacefully. Thursday morning Joe helped with breakfast, and then left for the church. Kate cleaned up breakfast and then got the kids all dressed. It was a lovely day and she wanted to take the kids out in the yard. With the resilience of a child, Buddy seemed to be regaining strength quickly. It was then she realized Buddy didn't have any shoes. She weighed her options. She could wait until this evening when Joe was home, but her parents were coming for dinner. Joe was supposed to work at the church tomorrow, so he wouldn't be around then either. She could leave Abby at Jenny's, or she could take all the kids to the store with her. She knew the store had shopping carts that had seats for two and she could put Grace in the back of the cart in her car seat. However, how was she going to get from the van to the store? She decided to try it. She could park next to the cart return rack. If there was a two-seater in the rack, she was all set. If not, she could put Buddy in the seat, Grace in the back, and carry Abby and push the cart with one hand from the van into the store where she could switch carts. She could also pick up a few more outfits for

Buddy while they were there. As she packed the diaper bag including snacks and two pink sippy cups, she added blue sippy cups to her list.

She debated how to get all three kids to the van. She muttered to herself that new shoes would simplify the process as she could then let Abby and Buddy walk with her to the van. She finally took all three kids out on the porch. She signed to Abby to go to the van, picked up Buddy and grabbed the handle of Grace's car seat, and headed to the van. As she was buckling all three kids into the van, she made a mental note that she needed to add extra time to her schedule when going anywhere, if she ever wanted to be on time again.

As she pulled into the parking spot next to the cart return rack, she was relieved to see a cart with two seats in the rack. Her shopping went well. Grace had fallen asleep in the car and slept the whole time they were in the store. Abby and Buddy entertained each other and rode along in the cart happily. Kate soon had selected Buddy's new sneakers and a pair of shoes for church as well as several new outfits. She could see that Buddy was tiring. This was the longest he'd stayed awake. Kate checked out and buckling the kids into the van, headed for home. She left the purchases in the van, except for Buddy's new sneakers that were already on his feet. She got all the kids out of the van and told Buddy and Abby to go to the house and picked up the still sleeping Grace. They got into the house without mishap, and she quickly got lunch on the table. She managed to get Abby and Buddy fed and down for their naps before Grace woke up. Kate cuddled Grace close telling her what a good girl she was. Grace's response was to let her mommy know she was a hungry girl. Kate laughed and settled into the rocker to feed her. With Grace fed and happily playing, Kate decided to mix up the meatloaf for supper and scrub the potatoes for baking while the older two napped. By the time she finished Grace was ready for a nap. When she had tucked Grace into her crib, she checked on the other two. Both kids were still sound asleep.

When the kids woke up, she explained to Buddy about grandma and grandpa coming for dinner. She taught him the signs they used for grandma and grandpa.

The afternoon went by quickly. When Joe got home, dinner was in the oven and all three kids were playing happily. Kate was having second thoughts about surprising her parents with Buddy. Joe offered to call Charlie and let him know as well as his parents. Kate felt relieved and agreed to Joe calling. He left a message for Charlie but was able to reach his parents. They were thrilled with the news. When he got off the phone with his parents, he found a text from Charlie saying he got the message and would see them soon.

Joe was in the living room with Abby and Buddy when he heard Ruth and Charlie come in the kitchen door. He heard Ruth talking to Kate and then noticed Buddy standing stiff as a board his eyes wide staring at the kitchen door.

Joe moved to pick him up talking soothingly saying, "Buddy, it's grandma and grandpa. Mommy told you they were coming. Nobody is going to hurt you." Buddy remained stiff in Joe's arms while he was talking. Then he struggled to get down. As soon as his feet were on the floor he took off like a shot towards the kitchen. Kate saw him stop in his tracks at the door of the kitchen his eyes wide.

Ruth's back was to the door. Seeing the look on Kate's

face she turned around and said, "oh my, Buddy." In an instant, he was in her arms tears running down both their faces. Kate turned to her dad and saw tears in his eyes also.

He said quietly, "we found him locked in the closet in unit one yesterday. He became attached quickly to Ruth and she stayed with him until Cheryl came in and asked her to leave so he wouldn't cling to her when the foster parents came. We knew you two wanted to adopt not foster so we never thought it might be you."

Ruth and Buddy had recovered their initial shock and Ruth was sitting at the kitchen table with Buddy in her lap. Buddy pointed to Ruth, signed "grandma", and pointed to himself.

"Yes, Buddy I am your grandma," Ruth signed and spoke. She gave him another hug and then said, "I think mommy has supper ready, shall we eat?"

After supper, Buddy took grandma to see his room. Charlie quickly filled Joe and Kate in on a little more of the happenings from the day before. When it was bedtime for Buddy, Ruth and Charlie decided to leave. They felt Buddy would settle better if they weren't there. They also wanted to be sure he knew they were leaving so he wouldn't expect them to be there when he woke up in the morning. They did tell him they would see him again soon.

29

Saturday there was such a marked improvement in Buddy's energy level they decided they would all go to church the next morning. They would decide whether to take him to Sunday School and children's church based on how comfortable he seemed with the separation from Kate and Joe. He could easily sit with them he was so quiet.

When Joe was putting Buddy to bed on Saturday night he asked, "have you ever been to church?"

Buddy nodded yes.

"Did you like it?"

Again, Buddy nodded and then signed "Jesus."

"Yes," Joe said. "We learn about Jesus at church. Tomorrow is Sunday and we are all going to church."

Buddy smiled and signed "good". Joe prayed with Buddy and gave him a hug. He sat on the edge of the bed a minute and debated. He knew that to adopt Buddy, they needed to find out who he was. He was doing so well that Joe didn't want to upset him, but he thought this might be a good opportunity to ask some questions. "Who took you to church?" Joe asked.

Buddy signed "mommy" and "daddy".

"Your mommy and daddy took you to church?"

Buddy nodded yes.

Since he didn't seem bothered by talking about his parents, Joe continued. "The mommy at grandma's and grandpa's motel took you to church?"

"No mommy, no mommy" he signed and looked ready to bolt.

"Hey, Buddy, it's ok, you are safe. Come here to daddy." Slowly Bubby lost the look of terror and came to Joe. He cuddled the small boy and talked to him soothingly until he felt him relax. He gently laid him down on the bed and covered him up. Joe kissed the top of his head and went to find Kate.

Joe found Kate in the bedroom feeding Grace. He filled her in on what had happened with Buddy.

"What do you think he meant?" she asked.

"I don't know," Joe said. "He was fine talking about his mom and dad. When I mentioned the motel, he kept saying no mommy. I think he might have been trying to tell us that the woman at the motel wasn't his mommy."

"Then where is his mom and who is that woman?" Kate wanted to know. They didn't have any answers. They both knew they were going to have to work on trusting God with Buddy's situation. They both loved him so dearly already. But what if somewhere his biological mom and dad were praying for him to come home?

Sunday morning when they got to the door of the two's and three's Sunday School room, Abby took Buddy's hand, and he willingly went with her into the classroom. Kate explained to the teacher that he was their foster son. She told the teacher that he could hear but didn't speak. The teacher assured them that Buddy would be fine. Joe and

Kate seeing that Buddy seemed comfortable, left to go to their own class.

At the end of Sunday School, they picked up the two children. As a two-year-old, Abby still went to the church nursery during the entire worship service. Grace was in the nursery as well. Buddy as a three-year-old would sit with Joe and Kate during the first part of the service. Then he would have the option to stay with them or go to a children's church program. As Kate carried him into the sanctuary, he seemed comfortable in the surroundings, as if he had attended a church service before. Kate's and Joe's family greeted Buddy as well as Kate and Joe. Some of the rest of the congregation asked Joe and Kate who he was. Soon the service started. Buddy sat cuddled in Kate's lap. When they stood to sing, Joe took Buddy into his arms. Buddy laid his head on Joe's shoulder and was soon asleep. He was still asleep when the kids were dismissed for children's church and Joe and Kate opted to let him sleep. As the end of the service neared, Joe handed the still sleeping Buddy to Kate and slipped out of the pew. He positioned himself at the back of the auditorium to greet people as they exited the service.

As Kate stood up at the end of the service, Buddy woke up and looked around. He immediately signed "Daddy" and Kate pointed to where Joe stood at the back. Buddy relaxed and looked around. Spotting Ruth and Charlie he broke into a grin. They had come in late, and he had already been asleep. He wiggled to get down and signed, "grandma" and "grandpa." Seeing that Ruth saw his intention Kate let him down and he was soon in Ruth's arms.

Kate made her way through the crowd to where Ruth

was still holding Buddy. "Can he stay with you while I go get Abby and Grace," Kate asked?

"Of course," answered Ruth, "we will meet you by the coat rack."

"Thanks," said Kate as she headed towards the door.

"Where's Buddy," Joe questioned as he saw Kate heading out the door alone.

"He spotted grandma," she answered with a smile.

Joe turned back to the people coming out the door and Kate went to the nursery. By the time Kate had the kids' coats on Joe was ready to go. Soon they were headed home with Nate, Jenny, and their kids right behind.

Kate had put a big pan of frozen ziti in the oven right before she left knowing it would be ready to serve when she walked in the door. As they walked in the door the tantalizing smell of the sauce and meat greeted them. Sammy announced, "I'm hungry, can we eat?"

Everyone laughed and Jenny said, "I'll set table while everyone washes up." Nate offered to supervise washing up and Joe took Grace up to bed. Jenny slipped Jackson into the extra highchair and started to set the table. In a short time, everyone was seated. Joe asked for the blessing and dinner was underway.

After dinner, the younger kids, Abby, Jackson, and Andy went down for a nap. Nate and Joe took Buddy and Sammy out to play in the yard. Joe had asked Kate, "is Buddy going down for a nap or not."

Kate looked at Buddy playing with Sammy and said, "he seems okay for now. Let's let him go out and play. Keep an eye on him and if he starts to tire, I'll put him down for a nap. Maybe the nap during church will be enough."

Joe asked, "Buddy do you want to come outside and

play?" Buddy pointed to Sammy. "Yes," Joe assured him, "Sammy is coming." Buddy grinned and nodded yes.

While the men were outside with the kids, Jenny and Kate did the dishes, cleaned up the kitchen, and talked. Jenny asked, "Do you think Buddy can talk?"

"I don't know," Kate responded. "We haven't heard him make any sounds."

"Have you been able to find out anything about who he is?" Jenny asked.

"Last night when Joe put him to bed, he told Joe that he went to church with his mommy and daddy. When Joe asked if his mommy at the motel took him to church, he panicked and signed repeatedly no mommy. I don't think the woman at the motel is his mother."

"Have you told Cheryl?"

"It's on my to-do list for tomorrow morning. It's a little scary." Kate continued. "If that woman is his mother, we stand a good chance that he will be freed. If she's not, then maybe his mother is looking for him. As loving as he is, somebody loved that little boy."

Jenny said, "but you said Cheryl checked for missing children?"

"She did," Kate said, "that's what's strange. If that wasn't his mother at the motel, how did she get him?" Neither of the women had any answers, and since the dishes were finished, they headed to the dining room table.

Every year the Kanells and the Landers had family photos done the first weekend in November. They always planned an elaborate clothing scheme. Nate and Jenny and their kids were to be included this year for the first time. The big picture day was the topic of conversation whenever two or more of the women got together. No one had any ideas about what to do this year. One year they had all dressed in clothing from the early 1900s. One year everyone wore overalls. Jenny had been thinking about it and said, "what if everyone wore jeans and color-coded turtlenecks?"

"Color-coded turtlenecks?" Kate asked confused.

"Yeah," Jenny continued, all the Kanells, both those by birth and those by marriage wear red turtlenecks, all the Landers can wear green."

Kate squealed, "I love it but let's take it one step further. Each individual family can wear matching vests. We always take pictures of everyone all together, each family, and one of just the kids. Anyone looking will be able to tell who belongs to who."

"Do you think the others will like it?" asked Jenny.

"I think they will be so relieved to have a plan they wouldn't care if we all had to wrap up in duct tape," Kate said with a laugh.

Jenny joined her in laughter. Then she thought of something.

"What color turtleneck will you and Joe wear? And the kids?"

Kate pondered for a moment. "Joe and the kids will wear red. I'll wear green. My vest will identify me with Joe and the kids." Jenny looked out the window to see how things were going in the yard. She could see the kids playing happily. Kate went upstairs to check on the kids and came back with Grace reporting all the others were still asleep.

Jenny said, "Sunday morning tends to wear Andy and Jackson out."

"Abby too," Kate said. Jenny went to the computer to

177

see what she could find in vests that spanned all the sizes they would need. Kate angled the rocking chair so she could see the computer screen and settled down to feed Grace.

Forty-five minutes later the little kids were all up, Nate, Joe, and the big kids had come inside, and Kate and Jenny had found a place where they could get fifteen different styles of holiday vests in sizes from newborn to four xl. With a great sigh of relief, Kate put Grace in her swing and went to serve cookies and milk for an afternoon snack.

After the snack was done, Kate got out crayons and coloring books, puzzles and blocks and the kids were soon busily playing. Jackson who kept knocking over everyone's buildings had been banished to the playpen. He had protested briefly but soon became occupied with the toys in the playpen and peace reigned. The men had gone into the living room to check football scores. The women were keeping watch on the kids and talking about plans for the big picture day. One minute everyone was playing nicely, and the next minute Buddy and Sammy were fighting. Sammy was howling in pain from having his hair pulled by Buddy. Buddy had tears running silently down his cheeks from being punched by Sammy. The men hurried into the room just as the moms each picked up their sons. Kate said, "Joe and Nate will you keep a watch on the kids while Jenny and I take these two upstairs to figure out what happened?"

"Sure," the men answered.

Kate and Jenny took both boys into the jungle room upstairs. Kate started, "Buddy, what happened?" Buddy tried using his limited signing skill to explain. He pointed to Sammy, then hit his own hand.

Jenny looked at Sammy and, "did you hit Buddy?"
Sammy hung his head and said, "yes."
"Why?" Jenny asked.
"He wouldn't let me help Abby build."
Buddy pointed to himself and signed, "help A."
"Buddy, were you trying to help Abby build?" Kate asked. Buddy nodded yes. "Boys," Kate said praying for wisdom, "Abby likes to build with the blocks. She doesn't need help with the blocks. I'm very proud of both of you boys for wanting to help Abby. And she needs both of you. She needs Sammy to be her friend and she needs Buddy to be her brother. I need you two boys to help me with Abby. Abby loves both of you, but if you two start fighting you will scare Abby. Do you want Abby to be afraid of you?"

Both boys shook their heads no, a look of devastation on their faces. Seeing the look, Kate softened and said, "she isn't afraid of you yet. You boys had such a good time outside I think you can be very good friends, and both be helpers for Abby. What do you say?"

They looked at each other and smiled a little. "I like Buddy," said Sammy. Buddy pointed to himself and held his hands out to Kate.

"Do you want to say you like Sammy?" Kate asked. Buddy nodded emphatically. Kate showed him how to sign I like you, Sammy. Then she said, "I have a new sign for you two." She demonstrated a sign. The boys both copied her and look to Kate for a translation. "This is the sign for friend," Kate said. "Something I hope you two can be." The boys looked at each other and signed friends again.

Sammy looked at his mom and asked, "can we go now?"
Buddy looked at Kate and signed, "play my room"?
Kate looked at Jenny and raised an eyebrow. Jenny

understood the question and gave a tiny nod of approval. "OK, boys you can play in Buddy's room but if there is any more trouble, you will both be sitting in time out." Sammy had spent time in time out and didn't like it. Kate asked Buddy if he knew what time out was and he nodded that he did. "Do you boys want to be in timeout?"

"No," said Sammy.

"No," signed Buddy.

Kate hid a grin, noticing Jenny turning away, and said, "then play nicely."

"We will," said Sammy.

Buddy simply signed, "yes". Without a backward glance, the boys started towards Buddy's room.

Kate peeked in as she went by a few minutes later to be sure the baby monitor was on. Buddy spotted her and touched Sammy's arm to get his attention and signed "A" and pointed to Kate. Sammy seemed to understand. "Aunt Kate, will Abby be okay if we play up here for a while?"

Kate said, "I will watch out for her. I'll call you if she needs you."

Both boys signed thanks and the moms went downstairs. Kate checked the baby monitor in the kitchen when she got downstairs, and the boys seemed to be having fun.

30

The rest of the afternoon passed swiftly. Before they realized it, it was 4:40. Nate said, "if we are going to make it to evening service, we had better get our gang rounded up and get home."

"I have a better idea," said Joe. "I need to be at the church at 5:30 for a pizza party for the teens. Why don't I call and order extra pizza? You know how the teens like the kids. Join us for the pizza party."

"You sure?" asked Jenny.

"Positive," said Joe. "After the pizza, the teens are doing their once-a-month teen worship service. The teens loved the worship we had around the campfire at camp and wanted to have a campfire every week. We compromised and we have a teen worship service at the church once a month. We put flashlights inside a tepee of wood to simulate a campfire. You are welcome to stay and worship with us or go to the regular evening service."

Jenny and Nate shared a look and Nate said, "we'd love to join you."

Kate turned to Abby and said and signed, "go to Buddy's room. Tell Buddy and Sammy to come to mom."

Abby happily went towards the stairs. The adults all eavesdropped shamelessly through the baby monitor.

"Hi, Abby," they heard Sammy say. Silence. They assumed Abby was signing. Sammy said, "we are supposed to go to mom. Okay, Buddy, let's go. Stop, what?" Sammy asked sounding as puzzled as the adults were. Nate headed for the stairs but stopped when Sammy said, "we need to pick up first? Okay, Abby, we will pick up and then go to Mom." The adults listening burst into laughter.

When Jenny could talk again, she said to Kate, "I guess you were right when you said Abby wasn't afraid of the boys!"

Joe called in the pizza order and then everyone went into action. By 5:15 they were all pulling into the parking lot at the church. A couple of the teens were already waiting and offered to help. Great timing said Joe, "there's the pizza. Can you guys help me carry it into the church?"

"Sure thing, Pastor Joe," they called.

Later, as they sat on the floor of the youth group room, around the wood and flashlight campfire singing praise songs, Kate's heart was full to overflowing. Grace was in her arms, but all the other kids were sitting in the lap of a teenager. Two of the girls were signing the songs for Abby. She praised God for the growth of this group spiritually and in numbers. When they had first come to this church the youth group numbered about eight teens. Most of them were there because their parents expected it. Tonight, she counted forty-nine teens. She knew that on an average non "campfire" night the group averaged about thirty-five teens. She knew Joe had been praying about the fact that if the group continued to grow and they hoped it did, he would need steady help, to be sure all the kids were being discipled properly. Joe planned to meet with Pastor Alan on Tuesday morning.

After service Kate and Jenny met up with Lydia, Leah, and Karen. They all approved the turtleneck and vest idea. Jenny had already offered to place the order if someone would get her all the sizes. The women went to gather their kids and husbands with promises to talk soon.

31

Tuesday morning Joe met with Pastor Alan and was pleased that Pastor agreed with the need to have someone work with Joe and the youth activities. Pastor Alan stated that Joe would continue to be the sole youth pastor for now, but he was to have a designated assistant. The plan was to ask a member of the church family to fill the position. Pastor Alan said, "I have my eye on someone, but since you will be directly working with this person, I'd like to hear your thoughts on a possible man first."

"My first choice," said Joe, "would be Nate Johnson. The youth know him and Jenny, and they interact well with the teens."

"Do you think he'd be interested?" asked Pastor Alan. "It would be a volunteer position at least for now."

"I do," said Joe. "The whole family came to the campfire with us last night. When I invited them, they jumped at the opportunity. I think the interactions were beneficial for all." Joe continued, "one of the teen girls who is very shy was talking to Jenny for about ten minutes. I think it was a desire to see Andy, who was in Jenny's arms, which motivated the girl to approach Jenny. Whatever the reason, Jenny was able to have more involvement with this particular teen in one evening than I have been able to have in the five months she has been coming to youth group activities."

"I'm glad to hear it," said Pastor Alan, "because Nate was my first choice also. I will approach Nate this week and ask him to consider helping regularly and let you know what he has to say."

With that, the two discussed a few other things and then Joe headed to his office to do some planning for upcoming youth activities. He had some ideas for outreaches that he hoped would draw more kids into the group that did not usually attend any church. He had been waiting to develop and carry out the plan because he knew it would involve a big-time commitment from him. With Grace's early birth and the restrictions placed on where she could go, then the unexpected move, there hadn't been time available. Now all Grace's restrictions were removed, so even with the addition of Buddy to the family, Joe felt he could move ahead with the plans. He was praying that Nate or someone would be in place to work with him by the time they were ready to have the outreach. Joe spent about an hour developing his idea and then spent the rest of the morning in prayer for the youth group members and his future assistant.

Kate spent the morning doing laundry and taking care of the children. Tomorrow was Buddy's appointment with the pediatrician. The appointment was at 9:00. Joe had arranged his schedule, so he was free until 1:00. The weather was supposed to be nice. Maybe they could take a trip to the park with the kids.

When they were putting Buddy to bed that night, they told him about the doctor's appointment the next morning. He looked a little concerned but when they assured him, he would come home after the appointment, he relaxed and cuddled down under the covers.

Wednesday morning Joe and Kate had not decided if they were both going with all three kids or if Kate and Buddy would go and Joe and the girls stay home. They decided Kate would go and Joe and the girls would get things ready for the park.

Kate had discussed with the doctor and Cheryl about Buddy's lack of an immunization record. The doctor had decided to give him some of the immunizations at this appointment. They would give ones that it was safer to redo than to be totally without them. Kate wondered if she should prepare Buddy for the immunizations or not. She opted to not tell him.

Kate took Buddy and left Joe trying to explain to Abby why she wasn't going with Mommy and Buddy. "Have fun," she called to Joe, "I'll pray for you."

"Thanks," he said.

Thirty minutes later Kate knew she was the one who needed prayer. Things had gone well at first. Buddy answered the doctor's questions with sign language. She asked, "can you talk?"

He signed "no."

"Could you ever talk?"

Buddy signed "yes". The doctor looked to Kate for help.

"Buddy," Kate said, "did you talk to your other Mommy and Daddy?"

He signed "yes."

"Did you stop talking when you were with your mommy and daddy?"

He signed "no."

"Did you stop talking when you were with the lady in the room where grandma found you?" He looked confused, so Kate clarified. "Did you talk with that lady?"

"Yes," Buddy, signed. "She said no talk."

The doctor said, "I am fairly certain the cause of his muteness is emotional, not physical."

Kate said, "I don't know why we never simply asked him before. Thank you, Doctor, this gives us some much-needed information and hope."

"If you have no more questions," the doctor continued, "I'll send the nurse in for the immunizations we agreed on."

"No more questions," Kate said.

The doctor turned to Buddy, "it was nice to meet you. Maybe next time I see you, you will have found your words."

Kate helped Buddy to get dressed telling him they were going to the park with daddy and the girls as soon as they were done. She was just tying his shoes when the door opened, and the nurse entered carrying the syringes. Buddy went ballistic. Terror was written all over his face. He was running around the small room as fast as he could go trying to stay out of Kate's reach. When she got him cornered, he was flailing and kicking. She managed to get a grip on him, but with his adrenalin pumping and giving him extra strength, she knew she wouldn't be able to hold him still enough to safely receive his immunization. She looked at the nurse and said, "I have an idea."

"Good," said the nurse. "Do you want me to leave for a minute?"

"No," Kate said, then mouthed, "please play along." The nurse looked quizzically at Kate until Kate said to her, "please go to time out in that chair now and stay there until I tell you." Understanding lighted the nurse's face and she went and sat. Then Kate turned to Buddy and said, "you go to timeout over there. I promise no one will give you your shot without telling you it's going to happen." Reluctantly Buddy went to sit keeping an eye on the syringes in the nurse's hand. Kate turned to Buddy who still looked terrified. "Buddy, these have medicine to help you stay healthy. Are you afraid they will hurt?"

"No," he signed and then continued with a combination of signs and pointing so rapidly that Kate got none of it after the no.

"Buddy," Kate said, "please slow down and try again. Tell me why you are afraid."

Buddy tried again more slowly. "Daddy go Jesus, Mommy sad, Mommy points to needles, Mommy go, no more Mommy."

Kate tried to sort it all out. "Daddy went somewhere? Mommy was sad? Mommy got shots? Mommy went somewhere and no more mommy?" Buddy answered each question with a yes. "And you are afraid if you get the shot something will happen to you." Buddy nodded his head as two big tears rolled down his cheek. "Come to mommy sweet boy," Kate said. He hesitated a minute, then he walked to Kate. She picked him up and cuddled him. "Buddy these shots will hurt a little when the nurse gives them to you. Tonight, your arm may hurt, but you will be all better in a day or two. These shots are good for you, the ones your mommy took were bad shots. Abby has had these shots. Grace had them too. They are both just fine. Now, are you ready for the nurse to give them to you? You can sit right here, and I will hold you while she does it."

Still looking very scared, he nodded yes and stretched out his arm expecting the shot like a drug user would do. Kate saw that the nurse noticed too.

"Okay," Kate said, "he is ready." Buddy didn't fight anymore, but she could feel him trembling in fear. When it was over, Kate walked out toward the waiting room. It hit her then, even with his extreme terror, he had remained silent. She began to wonder if he could talk. "Do you still want to go to the park?"

"What park?" he signed. She started to tell him the name of the park but realized he probably meant what is a park. As they left the doctor's office Kate explained what a park is. By the time they got home to pick up Joe and the girls, he had recovered from the terror at the doctor's and was excited to go to the park.

After the park, they went home for lunch. Joe made peanut butter and jelly sandwiches for the kids while Kate fed Grace. By the time Joe left for the church, the kids were down for their naps. Kate made a cup of tea and sat down to record the events of the morning in her notebook. They had been documenting every bit of information they could in hopes of finding out Buddy's real name.

Kate had already let Cheryl know that Buddy said the woman at the motel wasn't his mom. Cheryl continued to check databases of missing children. So far, he did not appear to have been kidnapped. This morning's reaction to the needles suggested his mother may have been an addict. Kate found it hard to believe that a child who was so loving hadn't been on the receiving end of love. Then she realized that she was being judgmental. His mother could have loved and cared for him despite a drug problem. Just because statistically, that wouldn't be the norm, didn't mean it was always the case. She thought about calling Cheryl but decided to wait. Maybe they could get Buddy to tell them some more. Cheryl was coming out to the house on Friday to check on how things were going. Kate would tell her then.

Kate wasn't sure what woke her at first. Then she heard it. A child was screaming, "you're not my mommy. I don't believe you, mommy's not dead. Mommy."

Joe was awake now, too. They both said, 'Buddy" at the same time and went running for his room.

Buddy was still screaming "You're not my mommy," when they entered his room. Kate picked him up and called his name. As soon as he was awake, he stopped screaming. Kate cuddled him close and talking softly assured him he was safe. Buddy relaxed in her arms. Soon he was sound asleep. She tucked him back in bed and followed Joe back to their room.

Joe glanced at the clock on the nightstand and saw it was 2:18. "Buddy can talk," Joe said. "Do you think he will talk in the morning? If he doesn't, should we insist he talks and not signs."

"I don't know if he will talk," answered Kate. "I don't think we should force him. We should let him know we know he can talk and encourage him, but not force it."

The next morning Kate and Joe were enjoying a cup of coffee and discussing what had happened the previous night. Just then they heard Buddy coming down the stairs. He came into the kitchen and Joe picked him up and said, "morning Buddy."

He hoped Buddy would talk but he signed, "morning daddy."

Kate said, "did you have a bad dream last night? Daddy and I heard you say, you're not my mommy. Was that the lady at grandma's and grandpa's place?"

Buddy signed "yes."

"Was she the lady that locked you in the closet?"

Again, he signed "yes."

"And she isn't your mommy?"

Buddy signed, "no, not mommy."

Joe asked, "do you know where your mommy is?"

With tears running down his cheeks, he signed, "with Jesus and Daddy."

Joe cuddled him close and said, "now you have a new mommy and daddy."

Friday when Cheryl came out for a required home visit, Kate told her about what had happened at the doctor's office. Kate also told her when they had talked to Buddy about his mother's needles, he had indicated that she gave herself the shots on her forearm. He had said the shots helped her feel happy. Cheryl asked Buddy, "where did mommy go?"

Buddy signed, "truck, light."

Kate thought a minute and then had an idea. She went up to the jungle room and looked through the books. Finally, she found what she was looking for. She took the book back down to Cheryl and Buddy. Buddy started looking through the book and about halfway through the book he got excited and showed Kate a picture. "Truck, light" he signed pointing to an ambulance.

"Did mommy go in an ambulance?" Kate asked.

Buddy copied the sign for ambulance that Kate had used. Then he signed, "Mommy go ambulance, no more Mommy."

Kate pulled him into her lap and said, "thank you for telling us." She cuddled him for a couple of minutes and then he slid off her lap and went to play with his toys.

Turning to Kate Cheryl said, "I am convinced that the woman at the motel was not his mom. What he said today may explain why he isn't in any of the databases. His mother may have overdosed, and the other woman took him. I have no idea why she took him, especially since she doesn't seem to have been very nice to him. How has his behavior been?"

Kate said, "he is a good boy. Very age-appropriate in his play. He is an active little boy and needs some reminders to put things away, but he is obedient and kind."

Cheryl asked, "no wild behaviors that would account for her locking him in the cupboard?"

"Absolutely none," Kate replied. "What happens if you can't find out his name?"

"We have to try for six months," said Cheryl. "If after six months we still don't have a name, we must advertise in the area newspapers for six months. At the end of that time, we can petition the court to terminate parental rights based on abandonment and you can adopt. However, if we go that route, you do run the risk that his mom or dad will show up someday with a story and try to convince a judge to overturn the adoption order. If the judge wanted, he could return Buddy to his biological mom or dad, and you would lose him."

"Then I guess we need to find out where his mother went," Kate added.

Kate and Cheryl made an appointment to meet the next month. Cheryl stopped by where Buddy was playing and got down on the floor near him. "I want you to try really hard to find your words and tell your new mommy your name. If we know your name, I might be able to find where your other mommy went. Will you try for me?" Cheryl asked. Buddy slowly nodded his head yes.

33

When Joe came home that afternoon, he told Kate, "Good news, Nate and Jenny have agreed to help with the youth group. I would like to get together with them every week to plan and pray. I bounced a couple of ideas off Nate and said I would check with you. Since Nate and Jenny won't be paid, the church has agreed to pay a babysitter for one evening a week for us to meet. Actually. they are going to pay for two teenagers since there are six little kids. We can leave all the kids either here or next door at Nate's. Or we can meet here after the kids are in bed."

Kate responded, "I would rather do it earlier. By the time the kids are asleep, I'm ready to relax, not to have a planning session."

Joe said, "Nate says he can get off early on Tuesday or Thursday. Does one look better to you than the other?"

Kate thought and said, "either one is fine with me. Would it be better for you if we met on Tuesday? It would give a little more time before youth group on Sunday to get things prepared?"

Joe responded, "most of the time I hope we are planning for youth activities that are several weeks out in the future, but just in case, let's plan on Tuesdays. What time are you thinking will work best?"

Kate did some figuring in her head. "What if we pick up the sitters at 4:30?" Jenny and I can alternate. One week she can cook for the kids, and I can cook for the adults. The next week we can switch. We could meet from 5:00 to 7:00 and still have the kids home and in bed by 8:00. Do you think 2 hours is long enough?"

Joe answered, "let's try it for a month. If we find it's not enough time, we can come up with a different plan. Let me call Nate and see if that works for him. Then I'll either play with the kids or help get dinner ready, your choice."

Sunday morning during the service an announcement was made by Pastor Alan letting the congregation know that Nate had agreed to serve as a volunteer assistant to Joe in the youth ministry. Pastor Alan announced that Jenny like Kate would assist as she was able but that both mothers' primary responsibility was to their families. He said that others were still needed to help, but that the church elders had felt that as the youth group continued to grow, another person was needed in a position as leader and part of the planning on a consistent regular basis. Nate was not going to replace any of the people who already helped regularly with the youth group activities. He also joked that if anyone wanted to support the ministry and didn't feel that teens were their ministry, they should talk to Kate and Jenny as between them the two couples had eight small children. Pastor Alan said, "that is another whole ministry." The congregation joined in the laughter. When the laughter died down, the song leader came forward to lead them in another song.

Kate whispered to Joe, "he said eight there's only six."

She turned around to try to find Jenny and Nate. There they were each one holding a little girl. Jenny had a big grin on her face. If anyone had asked Kate about the sermon that morning, she wouldn't have been able to tell them anything.

As soon as church was over, Kate headed straight to Jenny. "What's going on?" She demanded.

"This is Alexis," she said indicating the child in Nate's arms. "She is four. And I have got Nicole who is three. They arrived at midnight. Their parents were involved in a car accident last night. Mom died immediately. Dad made it to the hospital but is on life support. His condition has continued to deteriorate. They have not been able to locate next of kin. The police are getting a court order to search their apartment. There is still the possibility that they will locate the extended family. This could be a real short placement, or it could be permanent."

Kate asked, "were the girls in the car when the accident occurred?"

"They were all coming home from somewhere. They had suitcases in the car with them. We just need to pray for the girls. They don't understand what's going on."

"We will pray. Let us know if you need anything."

34

The next few weeks flew by. Joe and Kate had talked and decided to get a computer for Buddy and Abby to use with software that would help them with pre-reading skills. Buddy knew all his letters and the sounds. He was starting to spell both on the computer and with his hands using the manual alphabet. They wondered if he wasn't older than the three years he claimed.

Soon it was the first Saturday in November and picture day. The plan was to have everyone meet at the photographer's studio and do the group shots first. After all the groups had been done, individual families would be done. They had decided they would do the individual families in order from most kids to least kids and then individuals of the grandparents. As soon as the family was done, they were free to go over to Kate's and Joe's where they were all going to meet for lunch.

When they arrived at Debby's studio on Saturday, she was thrilled with the color-coded outfits. She asked them to all stand in family groups and then started to arrange them. Seating Ruth and Joy in the middle with Charlie and Dan behind them, she then started fitting in the families having parents each hold their children. She got a little flustered when she got to Joe and Kate because there were two parents and three children but when Joe swept up Abby and Buddy, one in each arm, she relaxed and said, "great." When she had everyone but Jenny, Nate, and their kids in she asked Nate and Jenny to sit on low stools in front of Ruth and Joy. Nate held Jackson and Jenny held Andy. Sammy stood between them, Alexis next to Jenny, and Nicole next to Nate. Debby started singing and acting goofy. The kids were entranced watching her and didn't realize she was snapping pictures the whole time. After several minutes she quieted down and called for everyone to look at her and say cheese. She continued to take several more shots of the group. Before anyone could start to get tired and fussy, she said "that's it for now." Next were shots of Joy, Dan, their kids, and grandkids, and then Charlie, Ruth, their kids, and grandkids. Then it was time for the pose all the parents had been dreading.

Debby didn't seem worried. She asked the parents to take the kids into the other studio which she had set up for the kids. The studio they walked into looked very strange. The whole floor was covered in black fabric that had mounds randomly placed throughout the entire area. The mounds turned out to be specially made infant and toddler seats. The photographer directed the moms to put the four babies in the infant seats, next Abby and Jackson went into the toddler seats. When they were all buckled in, she placed the four bigger kids. When everyone was in place, she flipped a switch and multicolored lights twinkled throughout the black fabric. She started snapping shots. After she had taken about twenty-five shots the kids started to wiggle. She quickly handed Kate a chart and said to look through the pictures on the computer and check off if we have a good shot of each kid. While the parents worked on that, she started juggling teddy bears to get the kids' attention. As soon as the kids had settled down to watch her, she let all the bears drop. When she bent to pick them up, she slid a pedal out in front of her. She started juggling again and snapping more shots. "How's it going?" she asked the parents.

"We have good shots of everyone except Abby."

"Which one is Abby?" Debby asked. Kate pointed her out. "Abby," Debby called to get her attention.

"She has trouble hearing," Kate informed Debby.

"Okay, we try something else," Debby said. She grabbed a flashlight out of a basket that was nearby and shined it at the spot where Abby was focusing. Abby looked up to see where the light was coming from. When Debby had her attention, she dropped the flashlight back into the basket and grabbed two balls that lit up. She started juggling them all the while snapping pictures. After about fifty shots she asked Kate to check and see if there were any good shots of Abby.

Kate said, "there are several good ones."

"We are done here then," said Debby. "I have enough shots of these guys. Computers are wonderful. Instead of trying to get a great shot that has everyone looking, I take fifty or more in the same pose. Then I can edit them all into one great shot." After that, they finished quickly and by 12:30 the last family was on their way to Kate's and Joe's.

35

NOVEMBER 21, 2011

Ruth and Charlie had added a large family room to their apartment and wanted everyone to come to their place for Thanksgiving. Kate, Joe, and the kids hadn't been to the motel since Buddy's arrival. They didn't want to scare him by taking him there. Ruth and Charlie understood and had made frequent visits to Joe's and Kate's house. Kate and Joe had promised to discuss it and decide tonight.

Kate wasn't surprised to find Joe waiting in the kitchen when she came down from putting Grace to bed. He had two slices of pie leftover from dinner and two glasses of iced tea sitting on the table waiting. Kate joined Joe at the table and slipped her hand into his. He bowed his head and asked God for wisdom, thanking him also for the gift of family.

Kate waited for Joe to start. She had shared with him earlier in the week that she missed being able to pop into her parents' home with the kids. She wanted to hear Joe's thinking first because he tended to be more logical while she thought with her heart. Joe simply said, "I think we should go on Thursday."

Kate closed her eyes and whispered, "thank you, Jesus." Opening her eyes, she looked at Joe and said, "do we tell him ahead of time?"

Joe was silent a moment and then said, "yes, we tell him in stages. We talk all week about going to grandma's and grandpa's. We don't remind him they live at the motel until Wednesday night."

Kate slowly nodded, "you're right, he should know before we go. And if he can't handle it?"

"We come home and try it again in a few days," Joe said. "Christmas was at my parents' last year so we will be at the motel for Christmas this year. I want his first Christmas in the family to be a celebration with the family."

"I love you," Kate said.

"And I love you," Joe responded. They finished their snack, put the dishes in the dishwasher, and started upstairs both praying for Thursday.

Buddy was excited to be going to grandma's house. He had gotten his cast off on Monday and couldn't wait to show everybody. Wednesday night Joe asked Buddy, "Where are we going tomorrow?"

He signed, "Grandma's and grandpa's house."

"Do you remember where they live?" Joe continued. He shook his head no. "Remember when grandma and grandpa found you in the closet?" Joe prompted. Slowly Buddy was connecting and nodded his head. "Grandma and grandpa live there, too. The lady who locked you in the closet is gone. No one will hurt you," promised Joe.

"Daddy hold me?" signed Buddy.

Joe asked, "now or tomorrow?"

"Tomorrow," Buddy signed.

"Of course, I will hold you tomorrow. But I'd also like

a hug tonight." Buddy shot into Joe's arm and Joe cuddled him close for several minutes until he felt the tension leaving Buddy's little body. He gently eased him down onto the bed and prayed with him. Then he tucked him in and said, "good night, I love you."

Buddy signed, "I love you" and rolled over to go to sleep.

When Joe checked him 15 minutes later, he was sound asleep. Joe continued to pray about the next day and even went as far as to put out a fleece before the Lord. He prayed, "Lord if you don't want us to do this, please give us a sign. Let someone be sick if this is the wrong decision. Amen"

Thursday morning no one was sick, so Joe took that as a sign that they should indeed go. They were supposed to be there at 11:00. Sensing that Buddy was too tense to wait, Kate called her mom around 9:00 and asked if they could come early.

Ruth said, "of course, come whenever you want." Kate and Joe finished getting everyone ready and 15 minutes later they were loading the van.

Kate's heart was breaking at the terror in Buddy's eyes. She looked at Joe and knew he had seen it too. She mouthed, "are we doing the right thing?"

He replied, "I think so." Kate texted her dad and asked him if he could come to the van and get the girls so they could deal with Buddy's terror.

He texted back, "of course. I'm already outside. I just spoke to the family in unit one where Buddy was found. She said to feel free to bring him in to see that the woman and the lock are gone."

When they arrived at the motel, Charlie came out and took the girls inside.

Buddy sat in his car seat staring at the first unit making no move to get out. "Buddy," called Joe. No reaction. Joe touched Buddy's hand gently and Buddy jumped. "Buddy," Joe called again, "look at Daddy." Slowly Buddy pulled his eyes away from the door to unit one and looked at Joe. "Remember what I told you last night?" Joe asked.

Buddy shook his head no.

"She's gone and I won't let anyone hurt you. You asked me to hold you. I'm going to take you out of your car seat now and hold you." Joe did what he had said. Buddy clung to Joe. Behind Buddy's back, Kate and Joe were communicating with looks and Kate's signs. Joe told Buddy, "I want you to see that she isn't here anymore. We are going over there and look."

Buddy trembled. Oh, he wanted to believe his daddy. Daddy had never lied to him. He buried his face in Joe's shoulder.

When they got to the door, Kate knocked. Buddy heard the door open and a women say hello. Kate introduced herself. The woman said, "Charlie told me about your little boy." Buddy was listening. The woman at the door didn't sound like She. He turned his head so he could peak at her. It wasn't She. He relaxed a little but still held tightly to Joe as he went into the room and walked to the cupboard where She had always locked him up. There was no lock! Buddy looked closer. There was no door! No one could lock him in there again. He picked up his head and looked around. He could tell it was the same place, but it sure looked different than when he stayed here with She.

Joe walked through the whole unit. Buddy could see that She was no longer there. Joe could feel the tension leaving his little body.

Buddy looked at Kate and signed "all gone".

"Yes, Buddy," Kate answered, "She is all gone. Are you ready to go and see grandma and grandpa?"

"Yes," Buddy signed. Then turning to Joe, he signed "down Daddy." Joe put Buddy down and thanked the woman and followed his son out the door.

The rest of the day was a good time of fun with the family. The family was enjoying watching Grace respond to sound. Kate and Joe watched Buddy carefully, but he seemed totally relaxed and enjoying himself with the other kids, especially Sammy. The two had formed a close bond and often asked for playdates. She wished she knew Buddy's birthday. He had told them he was three. But he seemed to be more on level with Sammy who had turned four in September than Nicole who was three. They still watched over Abby but didn't tend to hover. Kate was glad as she didn't want Abby to be smothered.

It was past the kids' bedtime when they got home and the tired kids settled quickly, something for which Joe and Kate were grateful. Joe spent a little time making some notes regarding the big outreach that they were planning for the youth group over the Christmas break. At one point this afternoon Nate, Joe, Kate, and Jenny had all found themselves sitting around the kitchen table and had started talking about the upcoming outreach. As other members of the family came and went, several offered some good ideas. Joe wanted to write them down while they were still fresh in his mind. Kate and Joe hadn't slept well the night before with concerns about Buddy's reaction to the motel. When Joe woke up at two am Kate was awake and the two had spent time in prayer. They hoped to get in a little early tonight. He didn't have to work tomorrow, and they hoped that with a late-night the kids would sleep in, but they couldn't count on it. By 10:30 Joe and Kate were sound asleep.

Kate sat up quickly. What time was it? What had woken her up? The clock on the nightstand read 1:12. She was awake enough to remember she had heard a child yelling in terror. Must have been a bad dream, she thought. She cuddled back down under the blankets.

Joe pulled her close. "You okay?" he asked sleepily.

"I'm fine," she answered, "just a bad dream about a child yelling." Just as she closed her eyes she heard the cry again, this was no dream.

A child was screaming and crying in terror, "no don't, please don't lock the door." They were both on their feet and heading to Buddy's room. He was still asleep and calling out in his sleep.

Kate went to him and gently shook him. Buddy, you were having a dream," she said.

His eyes tried to focus on Kate. She cuddled him close, and he started to relax in her arms.

She said, "Buddy, you yelled out and talked in your dream. Daddy and I both heard you."

Buddy jumped as if he'd been slapped. He pulled away from Kate and went and curled up as small as possible in the corner. Kate started to go toward him but could see that he was terrorized. Not wanting to frighten him anymore, she sat on the edge of the bed. Joe stayed in the doorway and remained silent. He too didn't want to add to Buddy's fear.

Kate started to talk to him very softly. "Buddy, Daddy and I both heard you talk. We are happy to know that you can talk. We hope that soon you will use your words to talk to us. But it's ok if you want to sign for a little longer. Signing is good because it lets you talk to Abby. But you don't know all the words in sign that I think you could speak. Look at how much Sammy can say."

Kate and Joe noticed that he was no longer curled in a little ball. He seemed to be taking in what Kate was saying. "We love you, Buddy. We hope that one day soon you'll be able to use your words and tell us what we need to know to be able to make you our little boy forever. But if you can't, we will still love you and try to find a way to make you our boy forever."

Kate saw that he seemed to be over his fright, so she said, "come to mommy now Buddy." She held her breath as he sat there thinking. Then he crawled over to Kate. She picked him up and cuddled him for several minutes. She held him and sang Jesus loves me. Then she tucked him into bed and said, "I love you Buddy, and will always love you."

She went back to bed then and cuddled up to Joe who had slipped out after Buddy had climbed into Kate's lap. "He can talk Joe," she said. "Physically he can talk. Now we know that we just have to keep loving him and wait for him to trust us enough to talk to us."

Joe started praying to thank God for Buddy and asking for wisdom in helping Buddy begin to talk again. Kate was almost asleep when Joe whispered, "do you think he'll talk in the morning?"

When Kate woke in the morning, Joe was already up. She listened carefully and could hear Joe talking to

Buddy in his room, but no child's voice. She heard Joe ask Buddy if he wanted pancakes or waffles. She didn't hear Buddy respond, but she heard Joe say, "waffles it is" so she assumed Buddy had signed.

She got up and got dressed. When she got downstairs, Joe was mixing up the waffles with Buddy's and Abby's help. She looked to Joe hopefully and he shook his head no. Buddy still wasn't talking.

36

Sunday night at youth group Joe announced the plans for the Christmas break outreach. He said, "It's a four-day event. Christmas is on a Sunday so you will have the whole next week off from school. We will meet at the church at 1:00 pm on Monday, December 26. We will travel by coach bus to a Christian college arriving at about 4:00. We will join four other youth groups. Monday night we will have some special activities including a worship service. Tuesday we will have seminars about walking with Jesus, sharing your faith, personal Bible study, missions, and many more. That night we will attend a concert with a nationally known Christian recording artist. Wednesday morning, we will meet to hear the plans for a special event. The college is hosting a special event for underprivileged kids, and we are going to help. You will each be paired with a younger child for the day, and you will take part in the planned activities during the day. After the kids leave there is a special activity planned for the teens attending the event. Thursday morning, we have a wrap-up session and head home. The cost for the trip is $75 plus $25 for the bus. This is designed to be an outreach. Our goal is to take at least one hundred teens. If we have 100 teens, the bus is free. For every friend you bring who does not attend church anywhere you get a $50 discount. For every friend you bring who does attend church but not this church you get a $25 discount. And your guests do not have to pay. If you invite more than two friends, you can offer your discounts to a friend. At our last indoor campfire, we had forty-nine teens. If every one of those forty-nine teens came and brought one friend, we would have ninety-eight teens. Tonight, we have thirty-seven teens. If you each brought two people at least one unchurched, we would have our one hundred teens. Any questions? There were no questions, so he had them turn to Matthew *28:18-20*."

Then Jesus came to them and said, "All authority in heaven and on earth has been given to me. Therefore, go and make disciples of all nations, baptizing them in the name of the Father and of the Son and of the Holy Spirit, and teaching them to obey everything I have commanded you. And surely, I am with you always, to the very end of the age."

"Does anyone have a Bible that says go if you want to or it would be nice if you could preach the gospel? No of course you don't. Because this is a command, Go and preach. Not a choice. Some things in the Scriptures are very clear that we don't have a choice. Verses like do not steal, do not murder. No Christian thinks they are optional to obey. So why do we think it is optional to go and preach? It is not an option if we want to live in obedience to God. I think God honors your efforts if you bring others to a place where they can hear the salvation message preached, even if you yourselves aren't doing the preaching. So, I'm asking each one of you to pray about coming. If you aren't participating in the outreach by coming and bringing a friend or two, then how are you fulfilling the command to go and preach the gospel?"

On Friday, December 12th Joe was in his office at the church. He had just hung up a phone call from a family with three teens. The family had never been involved with any church before. A teen who regularly attended had invited them and the mom had called with questions. Joe had spent an hour on the phone with the mom answering questions about not only the outreach but also spiritual questions for the mom. In the end, the teens were registered for the outreach and the mom was going to talk to her husband about coming to church on Sunday. Joe made a note to mention the woman to Jenny. The woman, like Jenny, had had a traumatic birth experience that made it impossible for her to have any more children. Thirteen years later the woman was still suffering emotionally. Jenny was sensitive enough to the Lord's leading that Joe could mention the woman without sharing personal details, and Jenny would make the contact. As he added the three teens to the list, they brought the total to 101 teens registered for the event including thirty-eight who had no contact with any church. Joe called to confirm the coach buses.

Joe was pleased that everything was in place. When they had met this past Tuesday, Kate and Jenny had decided to not attend the event. Even though the college was running the event, Joe and Nate would be involved and busy most of the time. The two women decided that with eight small children they wouldn't be any help and it would be much easier to care for their children at home.

37

As Christmas drew near Buddy continued to increase his sign language skills but still had not spoken. He had had no more nightmares. As Kate thought about his calling out during his Thanksgiving night nightmare and his reaction, she realized his terror wasn't from the dream, but from the fact that he had spoken. They continued to encourage him to use words but had decided not to push. Something traumatic must have happened to frighten him so bad. They would keep loving him and pray that in time he would trust them enough to speak again.

On Christmas Eve the church held a special candlelight service. Many of the people that Joe and Kate had grown up with had moved away, returned to visit family, and were at the service. It was always a time of catching up on how friends were doing. Buddy was overwhelmed with the extra people and stayed close to Kate who was holding Grace. Abby was safe in her daddy's arms.

Buddy heard Kate say this is my foster son and thought who is Foster? He tugged on Kate's shirt to get her attention. When she looked at him, he signed, "who is fsr?" Kate looked puzzled. Buddy continued in sign, "you say my boy fsr to" and he pointed to the person to whom Kate had been speaking.

Understanding dawned on Kate and she asked. "do you mean foster?"

Buddy nodded his head yes.

"Can I tell you at home?" Another nod of yes and Buddy was content. He knew that it was mommy's and daddy's job to talk to people at church. He also knew his turn would come at home.

When they got home, Kate told Buddy to put on his pajamas and come to her room. She explained to Joe about Buddy's question. Joe took Abby to get her into her pajamas, while Kate got Grace into hers. By the time Grace was ready, Buddy was in the middle of Kate's and Joe's bed waiting. Sending up a prayer Kate began. "Babies grow in their mommy's tummy. Abby and Grace were once in my tummy. You were once in your mommy's tummy. Usually, babies and children stay with their mommies and daddies. When they can't, people like Cheryl find them new mommies and daddies. When they come to live with their new mommy and daddy, they are called foster children. Sometimes foster children go back to their mommy and daddy. Other times they get adopted and stay forever with their new mommy and daddy. When I told my friend you are my foster son, I was letting her know that even though you once had a different mommy, you were my little boy now. In Uncle Nate's and Aunt Jenny's family, Sammy was once in Aunt Jenny's tummy. Jackson and Andy came to them last summer. They had been in another mommy's tummy. That mommy died and can't take care of them. Aunt Jenny and Uncle Nate became their foster mommy and foster daddy. After Christmas, they will be able to adopt them and be their forever mommy and forever daddy. The girls just came to Aunt Jenny and Uncle Nate. They are their foster girls. We don't know yet if they will stay."

"Do I have to go?" he signed nervously?

"I hope not," Kate assured him. "Daddy and I want to adopt you, but before we can the judge has to say we can adopt you. Before he says we can, he wants to know who your first mommy and daddy were and where they are. The judge wants to know who the lady was that locked you in the closet and why you were with her. Cheryl is trying to find out. That's why mommy and daddy keep asking you to tell us your name. We want to find out who your first mommy is. Maybe she is looking for you. We need to find out where she is before we can adopt you."

Buddy thought about all Kate had told him. He thought about talking. There was so much he wanted to tell her. He knew his name and mommy's name. He knew where daddy was. But what if when he started talking, he talked too much and the bad men took him away. The She monster at the motel had told him if he talked, bad men would take him away to a bad place. He was a foster not a forever. He couldn't take the chance.

So, he tried to explain in sign. He wished he knew more words. How do you say ambulance in sign? Mommy had shown him, but he couldn't remember. He tried to explain. "Mommy sad. Daddy see Jesus. Mommy" - he pantomimed how his mother had used a needle for drugs. "Mommy go truck lights, noise, no more mommy. She take me. Grandma find me. You mommy now. You love me."

Kate said, "yes Buddy I am your mommy now and I do love you so very much. I told Cheryl that you said mommy got a shot and went in an ambulance. But where is she now? And now it is time for little boys to be in bed." Picking him up she carried him to bed.

At six on Christmas morning, Kate and Joe picked up the sleeping children and buckled them into the van. As Joe pulled out of the driveway Kate felt a small foot kick the back of her seat. She turned around to see what Buddy wanted. He signed "grandma?"

When Kate said "yes," he smiled and closed his eyes. Since the motel was only about 10 minutes away, he wouldn't get to sleep anymore, but Joe and Kate wanted to see his sleepy-eyed wonder of the Christmas tree surrounded by presents on his first Christmas with them.

And Joe prayed, "please Lord only the first not the last."

Joe and Kate were not disappointed when Buddy first saw the tree. Everyone except Nate and Jenny was already there. Nate and Jenny arrived right after them and for the next three hours, bedlam reigned at Ruth's and Charlie's. By 11:00 am presents were opened, hungry children fed, infants fed and put down for naps and the house and family room had settled down to pleasant busyness. Joe and Kate found themselves side by side on the couch in the living room. Joe took her hand and held it as they talked. The kids were busy with their new toys and all their cousins. "I know things were rather noisy this morning, but did you hear Buddy say anything?" asked Kate.

"Not a sound," Joe answered.

"I think it's harder to wait now that we know he can talk," said Kate.

'I know," said Joe, "but we have to remember it will happen in God's time."

"And if it doesn't happen?" Kate asked.

"Then we concentrate on signing and love him for who he is," Joe answered.

Kate sighed, "I do love him just like he is. He is so sweet. I guess my impatience comes from the fact I want to know for sure that there isn't someone out there looking for him. I trust God with Buddy. But if his will isn't for Buddy to be ours forever, I'm afraid my heart might break."

Joe squeezed her hand and said, "trust God with your heart, too."

"I know," said Kate, "it's just hard because I love Buddy so much."

"I understand," Joe said. "I thought very briefly about applying to be missionaries in deep dark Africa, where his birth family couldn't find us. But then reality set in and I realized we'd never be able to leave the country with him until he was ours. And if he was ours forever, we wouldn't have to leave the country."

"Good reasoning," Kate said laughing.

"So," Joe continued, "I guess I'll just stay here and do what God has called me to do."

38

The teen event went off better than anyone could have foreseen. They had had a total of 106 teens attend from their church. There were also just over 600 teens from the other youth groups. When they met after breakfast on Tuesday, Joe brought out a baby bottle of milk, a jar of baby food, and a cheeseburger left from last night's supper. He had explained that "to a new baby the bottle was wonderful, but when the baby got a little older it needed baby food. A newborn baby can't even handle baby food, while a seven-month-old baby needs more than just a bottle of formula. But neither the newborn baby nor the seven-month-old is ready for a burger like this. Everybody agrees that this is true?" Joe paused and saw heads all over the room nodding. "So it is in the Christian life. People who have not heard the message of the Bible, and who haven't accepted Christ are not ready even for milk. They still need to experience a new birth. Those who have trusted Christ so recently that they still haven't taken the next step need one kind of teaching and he held up the baby bottle. People who have accepted Christ and have started walking with him but know that they need to learn a lot more need a different type of teaching and he held up the jar of baby food. And those of you who grew up attending church and accepted Christ years ago need something tougher to learn and he held up the burger. Now I'm going to ask you to spend about 2 minutes thinking and praying. Those who have never made a commitment to Christ will be in the red group. Those of you who need the basics, and he held up the bottle will stay here, you are the blue group. Those who know the basics and need the next step and he held up the baby food are the green group. Those who are ready for meat are the yellow group." He gave them the two minutes and then watched as the kids lined up. Joe was pleased with the honesty of the teens from their youth group. As he watched them go, he didn't see too many going contrary to where he would have chosen. One of the girls, Sierra, who had been to teen camp last summer and came occasionally to youth group stayed in the milk group, when he probably would have placed her in the baby food group. One of the boys, Devin, stayed with his girlfriend in the baby food group when Joe knew he was ready for meat. But the girlfriend was very shy and a young Christian. Devin looked to Joe begging him to understand. And Joe did understand and was proud of him. When Joe smiled at him Devin returned the smile and continued after Nate who was leading that group. Joe made a note to catch up with Devin later and affirm his decision to put the need of his girlfriend above his needs. As he considered the outreach scheduled for the next day, he was glad the college students leading the event were in charge. They had 625 kids from five to twelve signed up to come for four hours. They had shared their plans with Joe, and he was impressed with their organization. He was even more impressed when the event was over having been a huge success with only a few minor incidents. Even in those incidents, God was in control. A five-year-old girl had spilled her juice all over her clothes at snack time. A youth group leader from another church had his wife and daughter with him and was able to change the child into clean dry clothes. The college students planned to follow up with the children in the weeks to come. He hadn't heard reports from any of the other groups but in their group, there were sixteen decisions for Christ and thirty-three kids had wanted to commit to Christ more fully. As they boarded the buses on Thursday afternoon Joe was physically tired. But was energized by all the Lord had done in the past few days.

JANUARY 4, 2012

Kate was awakened by the ringing of the phone at 7:00 am on Wednesday. She heard Joe say," that's great, she won't be happy with either of us if I don't wake her up for this. Kate," Joe called to her as he held out the phone. "Jenny wants to talk to you."

"Hello," said a still sleepy Kate. When she heard Jenny's excited voice she smiled. Jenny was a morning person.

Jenny didn't draw it out but shouted happily "we have a court date for the adoptions. There was a letter waiting for us when we got home last night. It's in 2 weeks on January 18th. Can you come to court with us? We want the whole Kanell/Landers clan there and then back to our house for a celebration."

"What time?" Kate asked.

"11:00 am," said Jenny.

"Okay, we'll be there."

"And Kate," added Jenny, "gifts aren't necessary, just the family to share in this special day."

"Okay," Kate agreed with Jenny already a plan forming in her mind. She would spread the word that Jenny said gifts weren't necessary and encourage everyone instead to contribute to a large playground set for the backyard to be installed as soon as the weather warmed up. Kate got up and dressed and left the room. Buddy and Abby were just waking up. Grace had eaten at 6:00 and gone back down for a nap. If Grace stuck to her normal routine, Kate had about 2 hours before she got up. Joe had mentioned last night that he planned to work on the computer at home this morning. She had agreed to handle breakfast, asking Joe to wake her up as soon as the kids got up. As she headed towards Abby's room to tell her to go downstairs, she saw Joe was already at work on his laptop in the Noah's Ark room.

Joe was a morning person who thought nothing of getting up at 5: 00 am and working on his computer for a while before the kids got up. He had started using the Noah's Ark room so he could hear the kids before they woke Kate. He had told Kate last week that as soon as Grace slept through the night, and they moved her into her own room he could use the small room off their room as an office.

It really could be anytime, thought Kate. Grace had been sleeping from 10 pm until 6 or 6:30 am for about a week now. When she did get up, she usually nursed for a short time and went back down until about 9:00. While Kate didn't like 6:00 am she had to admit the schedule worked very well. If Buddy or Abby were awake, Joe took them and gave Kate the time with Grace. By the time Grace woke at 9:00, Buddy and Abby were done eating and dressed. She usually had the dishwasher loaded and a load of laundry started. When Joe came downstairs for breakfast a half-hour later, Kate had it ready to go. After they had prayed and served the food, Kate asked how much work Joe still had to do on the computer.

"I'm done," he said. "Did you have something you wanted to do?"

Kate answered, "I thought we could move Grace into her new room. Karen is coming to play with the kids. With an extra person here, it's the perfect opportunity."

"Are you sure you're ready for Grace to move to her own room?" Joe asked.

"I don't know if I'll ever be ready," Kate answered honestly, "but Grace is ready." Joe took her hand and gently squeezed it to let her know he understood. While Kate loved Buddy, she was still sad when Grace passed each stage knowing that the likelihood of there ever being another baby in the house was very slim.

The move was accomplished in less than an hour. There wasn't much to do. The nursery/office room was small, so they had only put a crib and a changing table in the room for Grace. Most of her clothes were in the closet or dresser in her big room. Kate had only kept what she needed for the middle-of-the-night changes in there. Joe moved in a desk that he had been using in the Noah's ark room and a bookshelf from downstairs. While he got his computer up and running and his desk organized, Kate went to switch loads of laundry.

Then she checked on Karen and the kids. Buddy and Abby were playing a game with Karen that one of them had invented. Karen held a children's sign language book. She would say a word, Buddy would sign it and Abby would find it in the book. Then they would switch. Abby would sign and Buddy would find it. If Karen gave them a word they didn't know, she would teach it to them. Kate had been watching from the doorway for several minutes before anyone saw her. When Karen looked up and saw her Kate said, "looks like a fun game."

Karen said, "they know a lot of signs."

"They sure do," said Kate. "I think it's because we try to remember to sign when we are talking around them unless, of course, we are trying to not let them know what we are talking about, though Buddy is getting so good I often have to spell to stump him.

I think it's time to start lunch," Kate said and signed. "After lunch, Abby and Buddy will nap and I have a job for you. Can you stay until 3:00?" Karen said she could. Kate asked her to help the kids wash their hands and get them to the table while she reheated some leftover casserole. As soon as lunch was ready Kate stepped to the heating duct in the corner and called Joe. Seeing Karen's puzzled look Kate explained. "About three years ago my father had the heating system in this old house updated. My mom insisted this duct be left because it goes right up into the office and saves walking upstairs."

When lunch was over, Joe took Abby and Buddy to get ready for their naps and Kate took Grace upstairs to change and feed her. Karen volunteered to load the dishwasher.

Joe decided to spend some time working in his new office and Kate took Grace back downstairs with her. She offered to let Karen hold her while she got out the ingredients to make cookies. "Do you like to make cookies," Kate asked?

"Sure," said Karen. She put Grace in the swing and got out the cookie sheets. Kate and Karen were just pulling the last tray out of the oven when Joe and Buddy came into the kitchen looking for cookies.

"Is Abby still asleep?" asked Kate.

"Yes," answered Joe. "Buddy was starting to stir so I went in and got him." If Buddy slept for two hours as Abby did, he had trouble going to sleep at night. He wasn't ready to completely give up his nap for which Kate was very grateful. An hour was just about right.

After a snack of warm cookies and cold milk, Karen left for home.

40

Sunday night at youth group there were eighty-seven kids! Joe and Nate had prepared for a crowd, but this was unbelievable. Joe opened the meeting in prayer and then asked the kids to share what the Lord had taught them during the outreach event. Over and over the teens were mentioning the underprivileged kids with which they had worked. They wanted to do more. Could they see them again? What could they do for those kids? Joe was amazed and humbled at the response from the teens. He looked at them and said, "I don't know, but I will find out."

After that, several teens shared how it felt to lead someone to the Lord. One teen guy, Craig, shared that he was a loner. He had lived in eight foster homes in the last three years. His new foster parents attended this church, but he had refused to go to church with them and his caseworker had said they couldn't make him. He didn't think anyone even knew his name. But when Devin from school had invited him to come to the retreat and had known his name, he was struck speechless and nodded yes. Devin got him the information and called him three times to make sure he was coming. When he arrived, he was in Devin's group and Devin had introduced him to the others. After the concert, Devin and Pastor Joe led him to the Lord. For the first time in a long time, he felt like someone cared for him.

No one else said anything. Joe started praying, "Lord this is the way it's supposed to be, one Christian reaching out to a lost soul and showing them the way to you. Thank you for preparing the hearts of each teen who attended. We ask you to continue to work in each life and do great things in our area of the world. Grow these teens into the men and women of God who will continue to serve you. In the name of Jesus, Amen." Joe asked the teen song leaders to come then and lead the group in song.

From where she was standing in the back of the room, Kate could see Carrie's shoulders shaking as if she was crying. Kate was about to go to her when she saw two of the girls come up to Carrie. One of the girls put her arm around Carrie and then the three stood up and left the room. Just as the singing was ending the three girls returned with huge grins. Joe must have noticed the girls leaving and then returning. He asked one more time, does anyone else have anything to share?

Carrie stood and said, "I came to the event because I heard some girls talking and thought it would be a good way to get away from home for a couple of days. I wanted to ask Christ to forgive me and to be my Savior and friend. But I was afraid people would find out no one invited me. Then Pastor Joe invited me to come tonight. When Craig shared, I knew I had to ask Christ to forgive me, but I wasn't sure how. Then Paula and Cindy offered to pray with me. Tonight, I asked Jesus to be my Savior and to forgive my sins."

Joe said, "welcome to the family of God, Carrie." Joe

let his eyes look around the room and then said "there are eighty-seven teens here tonight. Look around. Nineteen teens who went on the outreach aren't here tonight. I know fifteen teens who were here attend different churches and that may account for some. Others may have a good reason for not being here. But I challenge each one of you to check on those who are missing tonight. Make sure they feel welcome in our group. Now let's close in prayer."

Since Joe had a deacon's meeting to attend after youth group, Kate didn't wait around but headed for home. She had just got the kids settled in bed when Joe got back. He peeked around the corner of the living room and asked if the kids were all in bed. When Kate assured him, they were, he came all the way in carrying two milkshakes. Kate squealed quietly with delight and asked, "how did the meeting go."

"It went so well that we need to celebrate." Joe continued to tell her, "the meeting was to discuss a proposed change to the budget. The deacons wanted to discuss adding either a paid youth worker or a minister of young adults. The board felt that the church could support one or the other but not both. There was an even split about which way to go. Then I told them Nate was about three weeks away from finishing his online degree in Biblical counseling. Nate and Jenny both desire to be in full-time ministry. They don't want to leave this church, and both feel committed to the youth group. I proposed that we hire Nate as a part-time youth worker and part-time minister to young adults. The looks on their faces said it all. They voted unanimously to offer Nate the job."

"That is fantastic! What an answer to prayer."

"We can't say anything to Jenny or Nate until the

church talks to him. The deacons are going to ask Nate to stop in after work tomorrow and they will offer him the position. They want him to start on February first. That will give him time to finish his online classes and give his notice at work."

"This is perfect," said Kate. "Let's invite them to dinner."

"That's a great idea," said Joe, "but I will do the inviting. You are sure to give it away if you talk to Jenny."

"I would not," protested Kate.

Joe started to laugh as Kate tried to appear to be offended and soon, they were both laughing.

41

Cheryl called on Tuesday, January 17. "I checked out the possibility of Buddy's mother having died from an overdose. There was only one person who died of an overdose within 200 miles of here who fit the age and ethnicity required to be Buddy's mother in the last eighteen months. A young woman named Kassandra Jones. But there is no way Kassie was Buddy's mom. Kassie was in the foster care system from the time she was six years old. She was a very troubled child and teen. At fourteen she got involved with gangs and ended up being stabbed multiple times. Her uterus was so severely damaged that it had to be removed. We are at a dead end. We need to push Buddy a little. Kids who enter foster care are required to have a review 90 days after they enter the foster care system. The caseworker goes before the judge and has to prove that everything possible is being done to reunite the child with the birth family or to prove cause for termination of parental rights. Buddy's review is scheduled for two weeks. The judge has the power to order Buddy to be seen by a professional therapist to find out the information. The judge who is scheduled to hear his review tends to not have a lot of sympathy regarding children who don't give information that is needed due to past trauma.

She feels that if the information is vital for deciding the long-term placement of the child, the child must be made to tell it. You and Joe will be gentler. Could you two try to push him a little? I need some kind of lead."

"We'll try," said Kate. "His signing is getting better. Maybe we can find out some answers."

"Thanks," said Cheryl "and remember sooner not later."

After the kids were down for a nap, Kate called Joe at the church and told him about the phone call. "I should be home around 4:00," said Joe. "Why don't we drop the girls off with my parents and take Buddy to the mall. You said the kids needed something new for adoption day for Jackson and Andy. We can stop for pizza and try to talk to him."

"Okay," said Kate, "I'll call your mom."

Buddy was thrilled to be going to the mall with Kate and Joe. Both of them were praying for a breakthrough. They had decided to shop first laying the groundwork for the conversation to come by talking about the upcoming adoption of Andy and Jackson.

They were walking down the center of the mall when Buddy stopped still for a second, then broke away from Kate and Joe and ran screaming "daddy, daddy." Joe and Kate were momentarily too stunned to react. Then they hurried after Buddy. Buddy ran as fast as he could towards a tall blond soldier. The soldier's back was to Buddy, and he didn't see him coming until Buddy wrapped his small arms around the soldiers' leg. With his small face buried in the soldier's leg, Buddy said, "Daddy, mommy said you went to heaven to live with Jesus, but I knew you didn't. I knew you'd come back for me and mommy." Kate and Joe had caught up to Buddy and motioned the soldier to be quiet. He looked puzzled but complied with their request. Buddy continued to talk, "you can help me find mommy. She got so sad when they said you were with Jesus. She took medicine and shots and got really sick. She wouldn't wake up. The ambulance took her away and I don't know where she is. Can you find her daddy?" Buddy looked up at the soldier and his face crumpled, "you're not my daddy." Kate moved in at that moment and wrapped a now sobbing Buddy in her arms. Joe and the soldier walked a short way away.

Joe said, "thank you so much for letting him keep talking. I'm his foster dad. He was found abandoned. He's lived with us for almost three months. Other than twice when he called out during a nightmare, that's the first he has spoken. We don't even know his name. We found out more in the last two minutes than during the last almost three months."

"No problem," said the soldier, "I'm glad I could help. Do you mind if I talk to him a minute?"

Joe hesitated and then said, "go ahead."

The soldier walked over to the bench where Kate was still holding Buddy. He continued to cry but his cries had again become silent.

The soldier sat down next to Kate and said, "Hey little buddy, I'm sorry I'm not your dad. I sure would be proud to have a special little boy like you for a son." Buddy turned his head slightly so that he could see the soldier. "Was your daddy a soldier?" Buddy nodded. "Did he go to the war?" Again, Buddy nodded. "Did a soldier come to your house and talk to your mommy?"

Buddy opened his eyes wide. How did he know a soldier came? Buddy nodded.

The soldier looked like he wished he hadn't started this but took a deep breath and continued. "Did your mommy tell you that your daddy was dead?" Buddy shook his head no.

Joe remembered what Buddy had said. "Did mommy tell you daddy went to live with Jesus?" Buddy nodded his head as two big tears rolled silently down his cheeks.

"Before the army sends a soldier to talk to a mommy, they make sure they know that the daddy is with Jesus. I know your daddy wanted to come home to you and your mommy as much as you want him to come home. But your daddy went to the war to make sure you would have a safe country to grow up in. Your daddy thought that was important. Sometimes daddies don't come back. Sometimes they go live with Jesus. I think your daddy would be happy to know you have a new daddy and mommy who love you. Maybe if you talk to this new mommy and daddy, they can help you find your other mommy."

Buddy had calmed considerably but was still somewhat shaken.

The soldier stood then and shook Joe's hand. "Thanks," said Joe.

"I hope it helps," responded the soldier.

As the soldier Joe walked away, Joe took a deep breath. Buddy's back was to him, so he signed to Kate. "Now what? Home?"

Kate shook her head no.

"Shopping?"

Again, no.

"Pizza?"

This time Kate nodded yes.

Joe said, "Buddy, let's go get some pizza." He picked

up his son and headed to the food court glad the soldier had gone the other direction. When they had their food, Joe prayed.

As they started eating, Kate said "Buddy we both heard you talk. We know you can use words to talk. You know that soldier was right. If we knew your name and mommy's name, we could try to find her. Cheryl has been looking, but with no names, it's very hard. Do you know mommy's name?"

He slowly nodded his head.

"Can you tell me her name?"

He opened his mouth and Kate and Joe held their breath.

Then he closed his mouth and shook his head no.

"Can you spell her name?"

He signed a "K."

"Did you know the name of the lady at grandma's motel?"

A look of fear crossed his face, but he nodded and signed, "Aunt K."

"What about you? What is your name?" Kate asked and held her breath.

He signed "B-u-d-d-y."

"Okay Buddy," said Joe. "Enough questions for now. Let's eat, we still need to get you new clothes for Jackson's and Andy's adoptions."

They finished their pizza and then went shopping. Kate quickly picked out the clothes for the three kids for the next day.

They had planned to stop at the grocery store on the way home. Buddy was so obviously exhausted from his emotional outburst that Joe suggested he drop off Kate and Buddy at the house first. He would grab the groceries and pick up the girls from his parents' house. Kate agreed with the new plan.

When they got home, Kate washed Buddy's tear-streaked face and tucked him into bed. When she turned around at the door to look at him, he was almost asleep already. Poor little guy, she thought. She stood watching him for a minute praying, Lord please help him to talk to us. Help us to know how hard to push. If it's your will, let us adopt him. It sounds like his parents may have been Christians Lord, but he talks like his mom was an addict. Please help Cheryl unravel this mystery. Amen

The courtroom was packed on January 18th, as Jackson and Andy became officially and forever part of the Johnson family. After they were done in court, there was a caravan of cars as everyone followed Jenny and Nate home. The mood at the house was very excited and happy except for Buddy who seemed subdued. Kate and Joe kept an eye on him. They tried to talk to him a couple of times, but he seemed to want to be left alone. They were the first to leave. They had let everyone know what had happened at the mall, so they all understood.

That night as they were tucking him into bed, Buddy signed, "me dop like Jackson and Andy?"

"Do you mean are you going to get adopted like Jackson and Andy?" asked Kate.

He signed, "yes."

"We are trying," said Joe. "We told Cheryl what you said yesterday. She is trying to find out where your mommy is. If you could tell us your name, it would sure help."

The look of sadness on his face nearly broke Kate's heart. She kissed the top of his head and left before she started crying.

Joe prayed with Buddy and then went in search of Kate. He found her in the kitchen looking out the window. He was sure she wasn't seeing anything. He wrapped his arms around her and reminded her, "we have to trust God."

"I know," said Kate. "But he is hurting, and I want to fix it for him, and I don't know how.

"Sure, you do," said Joe. "Keep loving him and trusting God who loves him more than we do."

42

Kate didn't sleep well that night. The next morning Joe was working at the church. He would be gone until early afternoon. Kate and Joe and the kids were having dinner with Pastor Alan and his wife and Kate was supposed to make a dessert to bring. The kids had been cranky all morning and Kate hadn't been able to get anything done. When kids communicate in sign, you can't multitask. When they asked a question, you had to stop what you were doing and turn to see what they were saying. Your hands had to be free to answer in sign. They had taught the kids to tug gently on their shirts to get their attention. Abby and Buddy had tugged on her shirt so often that day she wanted to yell don't anyone touch me. At least she would have nap time to get the dessert made.

But naptime was a disaster. Grace fell asleep while Abby and Buddy were finishing their lunch. Buddy fell asleep quickly, but Abby wouldn't go to sleep. By the time Abby was asleep, Grace was awake and hungry. Kate fed her and put her in the swing.

She had just gotten the ingredients out when she heard Buddy coming down the stairs. She gave him a snack of milk and a cookie, hoping to get her dessert made. When she heard him push his chair back to get down, she told him, "Go and get out a puzzle and let mommy finish this please. Thank you, Jesus," she whispered when he obeyed.

She was almost done when she felt a tug on her shirt. "I'm almost done, Buddy," she said without looking.

Again, the tug and then the voice they had so hoped to hear said, "Mommy, my name is Daniel."

9 781664 264908